BLOODLINE

The Legend of WindWalker

BLOODLINE

The Legend of WindWalker

CAROL COLSON

Author Reputation Press LLC
45 Dan Road Suite 5
Canton MA 02021
www.authorreputationpress.com
Hotline: 1(888) 821-0229
Fax: 1(508) 545-7580

Ordering Information:
Quantity sales. Special discounts are available on quantity purchases by corporations, associations, and others. For details, contact the publisher at the address above.

Printed in the United States of America.

ISBN-13:	Softcover	978-1-64961-698-2
	eBook	978-1-64961-699-9

Library of Congress Control Number: 2021915739

TABLE OF CONTENTS

Here's what readers are saying about:
BLOODLINE
The Legend of WindWalker

"Carol Colson is a natural storyteller. In this captivating adventure, Nhaya's understanding of her heritage deepens, and you will be wonderfully transported to her side as she experiences an awakening to all that is accessible her as a result of her connection with the Great Grandfather Spirit. This tale is spun like a fine silken thread all the way to its inspiring and uplifting conclusion."

Beth Misner - Author of *Jesus and the Secret: Where the Word of God and the Law of Attraction Intersect*

Five Stars – "Riveting. This book had my attention from the very first chapter!"

Linda E. - Amazon reviewer

Five Stars – "I love this book! The twist was awesome. I didn't see it coming."

Bridget M. – Amazon reviewer

"This is a book that crosses the lines. It could be argued that the target audience is teenage and young adult. However, like the best books, this has appeal across the board. Bloodline: The Legend of WindWalker crosses those lines."

Jon C. - Goodreads reader

PREFACE

The Bonner General Hospital emergency doors burst open. Two burley loggers rushed into the hall, half carrying and half dragging a third between them; fear etched in their weathered faces. A terrified woman with her child rushed in behind them.

"This guy is bleeding, bad!" one of the loggers hollered. "His arm is barely hanging on."

"This way!" the orderly shouted. "Bring him in here." He pointed to a vacant room. "Get a doctor down here. Stat!" His voice echoed down the empty hallway.

The young mother stood frozen as she watched the two men carry her husband's limp form into the first open room. Her daughter's hand trembled in her tightening grip. She turned to her and spoke. "Nhaya," she began, her voice soft and quivering, "go out to the car and check on your sister. This isn't the place for you right now, and Megan cannot be left alone."

Nhaya stared into her mother's face and nodded. "Mom, what does 'stat' mean?"

"It means to hurry. Now, honey, please go back to the car and watch your sister." Miriam hesitated for a moment beside the open curtain, her heart pounding. She wasn't prepared for the sudden change in her husband's appearance. Pressing her hand to her lips, she muffled a gasp. Paul's usually handsome face looked sallow and gray—the opposite of his once ruddy hue. Everything else in the room became a blur. Her husband needed her, and she rushed to his side.

"Paul, it's me, Miriam. I'm right here." She gently squeezed her husband's hand. The makeshift tourniquet fastened to his upper arm was soaked through, bright red with blood. She was not aware of the crimson pool gathering at her feet. She bowed her head, remembering the prayer chants of her people and recited them to her husband, hoping it would soothe him.

"Ma'am, please." A hand pressed into Miriam's shoulder. The nurse's voice was commanding, yet gentle. "You need to step aside now. Let the medics do their job."

Miriam backed away but remained in the hall. Her frightened eyes never leaving her husband's face.

The attending physician turned to the nurse. "Get that blood type, now."

An alarm screamed. Miriam sank; she knew what that sound meant. Her husband's heart had stopped. The doctor put the stethoscope to Paul's chest. "Code blue!"

"Ma'am? Ma'am, please." The charge nurse touched her hand.

Miriam gasped. She covered her mouth with her hand to keep from crying.

The nurse beckoned her, "I need to get some quick information from you. It won't take long. I promise. Please, come with me."

Miriam allowed herself to be ushered down the hall to the admissions office.

"What is your husband's name?"

"Pa–Paul Winters," Miriam's voice broke. Hiccupping breaths racked her chest. She buried her face in her hands.

The nurse's voice softened as she slid a box of tissue within Miriam's reach. "Mrs. Winters, I know this is very painful, but I have to ask you just a few more questions. How old is your husband?"

"He's...he's thirty-six."

In their haste, the privacy curtain to Paul Winters's room had been left open. Standing in the curl of the drape, Nhaya stood, unnoticed. Her little sister was safe and asleep in the car. She just needed to know if her father was all right before she could go back. Stretching to her tiptoes to see over the backs of the doctor and nurses, she strained to see her father's face.

"Where is that cart!" barked a man Nhaya thought was the doctor. "Keep that hand respirator on him." The doctor's hands were covered with blood.

Nhaya dared not move. It was chaos, with machines being rolled in and out of the room and nurses bending over her father.

"Excuse me," she said into the chaos. "I just need to see my father."

Surprised by the child's voice, the nurse standing in front of her spun and pulled back the curtain. "You can't be in here." She ushered Nhaya out of the room by her shoulders and quickly returned to her duties. Nhaya stood in the hallway, forgotten. She turned away and walked the hall, searching for her mother. After several minutes, she decided to sit down in a nearby chair and wait for her mother to find her. Then they both could find him together. Her mother would insist on seeing him.

Paul Winters lay still, as if asleep.

"Hey, stay with me here, pal." The doctor tore open Paul's shirt. The message went out. Everyone stood back as the paddles were placed on his chest. "Clear!" The electric surged through the still form in hopes of restarting his heart. Still, the green line continued to crawl across the screen; Paul's heartbeat had stopped. Only a straight line remained. Several minutes passed with no change.

Finally, the doctor reluctantly turned off the heart monitor and pulled off his gloves. "He just lost too much blood."

Miriam's voice became stern. "I need to be with my husband! He needs me, now!" She had been patient through all the questions. Grabbing her purse, she stood up.

"Mrs. Winters, you can't see him. He is still being treated."

At this point Miriam didn't care about the rules. No one was going to prevent her from being with her husband when he needed her most.

The charge nurse rose from her desk and then sat back down. The attending physician was walking toward them. Miriam studied him. His was face grim, his head and shoulders down. She hoped for good news even as her heart feared the worst.

"Mrs. Winters"—he touched her shoulder— "I'm so sorry. We did everything we could. He just got here too late."

Miriam heard his words which seemed to be coming from a great distance. She tried to comprehend what the doctor was saying. "NO!" Miriam cried out, shaking her head. "No, you're wrong, it can't be true. My husband is too young to die."

Nhaya rubbed her arms, feeling the chill of the fall air. In the backseat of the old DeSoto, her sister Megan slept peacefully. She tucked Gretchen, Megan's rag doll, and her favorite blanket around her sister a little closer. For a moment, Nhaya enjoyed Megan's tranquility and was most thankful Megan didn't have to see all of this. Looking at Megan, Nhaya knew her sister would wake soon and that she'd be hungry. She had to find her mother. Nhaya closed the car door with care then sprinted back to the emergency's entrance.

Nhaya paused after the electric door to emergency closed behind her. She focused her attention down the length of the hall toward the main seating area in hopes of finding the two men who'd brought her father in. Sounds of business echoed behind curtained doors, but she couldn't see anything inside the rooms. Biting her lip, she pressed on, determined to see what was happening with her father and when he could come home.

She spotted a familiar face. "Where did my mother go?" Nhaya asked. "Where are the two men that brought my dad here?"

"What is your mother's name, hun?" The nurse began to search for the name on her chart.

"Her name is Miriam."

"Miriam? I don't see a Miriam here. When did she come in?"

"No, it's my dad you're helping. Paul Winters."

"Oh." The nurse frowned. "You better come with me. She is lying down."

Nhaya stepped away. "No, I have to go back to the car. Tell her my sister and me—we are waiting."

CHAPTER ONE

Three Years Later

*N*haya stared, out the bus window as if in a trance, The endless ribbon of highway lined by a thick row tall pines was something she always watched with excitement, but not this time.

Her mind pondered the dream again. It distracted her like the itch that could not be ignored; a puzzle she could not solve. After her father died, the dream became more frequent, and it was always the same until lately. An old woman stood, in front of her, in the dream. She seemed to have something important to say, but she always woke up before it was revealed. Lately in her dream, she found herself walking down a road that was painted red.

Then, she recalled the look on her mother's face when she left her at the bus depot to wait on her own. She knew her mother was still in denial about her father's death, but her sudden unbridled anger didn't need to fall on her shoulders again. She had won the argument with her mother this time, but something was different. She had become more unwavering. She knew her mother's anger would pass. she just had to accept it.

Nhaya's resolve stood and she pushed the guilt away. There was no way she was going to miss this year! Not even for her sister's sixth birthday. Turning six wasn't a big deal Nhaya had reasoned to her mother. Camp was necessary. To her it meant leaving her troubles behind and escaping into another world, if only for a week. Nhaya glanced at her father's watch. The turnoff to the summer camp on Highway 95 was just around the bend and so was the road sign directing newcomers to Camp Cocolalla. Just seeing the sign made her smile and trigger better memories Leaning across her uncomfortable vinyl bus seat, Nhaya picked up a magazine left by another rider, and began to fan herself. Needing a stronger breeze, she slid over and pulled down the window, pretending not to notice the disapproving glare from the bus driver. Why the stringent rule that windows must never be opened more than a crack, she never understood.

The bus pitched back and forth on the rutted road when it turned off the main highway. Nhaya steadied herself by grabbing the back of the seat in front of her until the bus lurched to a stop. Cheers and clapping rose from everyone. Her heart leaped, too, as it always did, knowing the fun and excitement that lay ahead.

Northern Idaho was a land of colors around her; green forests so thick that in some areas the sunlight couldn't even penetrate, and the blue-sky lakes surrounding Kanitsu National Forest were so plentiful, they would take a lifetime to explore. Best of all, Cocolalla was right in the middle of it all! To Nhaya, this was paradise.

Nhaya's fingernails tapped impatiently on the metal bar that ran along the top of the seat in front of her. After coming to a stop, the driver sat back for a moment, removed his cap, and wiped his brow. Finally, he leaned forward and pulled back the lever, and with a squeak and a groan, the door opened the way to freedom.

She wasn't the only one dying to start the week. When the metal door swung open, it was like a stampede as teens hurried to be the first out of the bus. She waited longer than she wanted to, then excused herself as she wriggled her way into the cramped line.

Away from the bus fumes, Nhaya smelled the familiar pungent scent of pine as she walked off main dirt roads into the trees. Fallen pine needles crunched beneath her feet and as she walked along an uncrowded path, she could feel her body relax forgetting the earlier argument with her mother. She let out a long sigh and smiled to herself. It was going to be a great week.

This time with renewed excitement, Nhaya looked at her father's watch that fit loosely around her wrist. The bus had arrived early so there was still time to explore. Reminding herself again of the time, and once camp officially started, it would be against the rules to leave the main campgrounds.

She hardly noticed the other campers picking up and unpacking their supplies. She tilted her face skyward, still able to see patches of blue peeking through the tops of the tall lodgepole pines; their lower branches were sparce and dead from lack of sunshine and nourishment. When she was little, her father tried to explain to her that cutting down the forest's sick trees helped to keep the other trees healthy.

The smoky scent of a recent campfire compelled her toward an empty campsite. Suddenly, the hairs on her arms bristled, chased by chills as she stepped away from the main path.

Nhaya found herself in the center of a vacant campsite with its well packed earth. She had just turned eleven when her father died.

Nhaya began to search the area hoping to find something—anything—that would show she had camped there before; perhaps a special pile of rocks she once gathered or the jute rope her father had tied high on a tree to secure his catch of the morning. Anything that could have remained. She sat down on a log, and in her mind, she began to set up camp as they had so many times before.

The small two-man tent would be their home for a week. It was staked down next to a tree for shade and far enough away from a campfire. Breakfast consisted of two small brook trout that were caught earlier. Her father never caught more than they would eat, and he always thanked The Great Spirit for providing for them Early mornings she would wrap herself in a heavy cotton Indian blanket with its colorful patterns and sip hot chocolate watching her father prepare breakfast. She laughed as she remembered how he always managed to burn his fingers pulling the tin pot of coffee from the fiery coals. And, she always told him, "Next time, Dad, bring the oven mitts." Which, of course, he never remembered.

Nhaya laughed out loud now at his silent swearing under his breath.

She enjoyed the nights the best. Cozy and warmed by the well-stocked fire, she watched her father act out the stories passed down through the generations of their tribe and many more from other tribes. Stories of Coyote, the wisest in the animal world, became her favorite. When other animals were in trouble, Coyote would always give them sound advice.

Nhaya picked up tree limb that had been left by the previous camper and sat down beside the fire pit. Gently poking the stick through the grey ashes, she was able to revive a small flame. It was simple to do, especially if the fire had not been properly doused, compared to the difficulty of starting a fire without matches or coals. She had watched in awe as her father vigorously rubbed two sticks together into a small pile of papers and sticks, first causing the paper to smoke and then— like magic—the spark became a small flame.

The main campgrounds of Cocolalla had indoor bathrooms and modern cooking facilities. Her father, however, felt that modern facilities didn't fit the life of a brave, so he chose the more remote sites for camping. On occasion, her mother would join them, but after Megan was born, her mother had stopped coming, saying it was too difficult to manage everything a baby needed in an isolated campsite with no amenities.

Nhaya and her father ate simply; one-pot stews with potatoes he brought from home and meat he hunted with his bow and traps. Together they picked herbs. Thyme and sage gave the stew a rich flavor. Sometimes he would tease her about making dinner out of ground up squirrel or red-tailed chipmunks, but she never knew if he was teasing. The rabbits were caught in a simple homemade trap. She remembered listening to the poor trapped animal moving about inside the long wooden box, then becoming silent as if accepting its fate.

A thought occurred to her. In many ways she had become like the rabbit caught in that trap. She had been frantically trying to bring back the past, reliving the memories as if she could make them happen again. Her father was gone. She couldn't bring him back, and she couldn't spend the rest of her life like she wanted to—living in the wilderness. But still, she refused to give up the only teachings that made sense to her. She flung the marshmallow stick into the woods. How could she follow in her father's footsteps if her mother kept her home?

Nhaya took a few steps away from the campsite to practice with her bow. Then, she remembered the small leather pouch she had hidden inside the pocket of her jacket. She couldn't wait to look at it again.

Nhaya pulled out the necklace. It was simple, made from a strand of rawhide strung through a hole bored through a piece of petrified bone and accented by a few small colorful beads, some of which were faded and broken over time. Nhaya carefully examined the piece of bone again and wished she understood the strange hand- carved markings that held a secret.

She clearly remembered the night her father had pulled the necklace from his shirt…

"This, Nhaya, has been passed down through many generations of our tribe. It will be yours someday; you must guard it with your life. It has great value," he had said.

She remembered her excitement. "When can I have it?" she asked.

"The right time will come."

The next day, she told her mother about the necklace her father had shown her. She hoped her mother could tell her something more about the writings on the weathered, but smooth bone. Instead, the necklace had suddenly disappeared from the house. She had forgotten about it until years later when she was in Montana visiting her aunt and going through her cedar chest, looking for more pictures of her father, that she saw the necklace.

"Nhaya," Aunt Bessie told her then, "this necklace was never his to give. And, it must be given, not taken. You have a sister, too."

Nhaya had appealed to her aunt. "Aunt Bessie," she cried, "my father already promised it to me. He told me to protect it. How can I do that if you have it? I will keep it safe at home." It was her birthright. Obviously, the necklace should be with her—not locked away in some chest waiting for some other right person to be chosen.

It was two weeks later during Montana's celebration week that a package arrived from their aunt. It was Megan's birthday present. Aunt Bessie had sent another quilt she'd finished. Her mother had taken the package with the necklace into her own bedroom. It was quickly in a small box with Megan's gift.

Nhaya sighed, coming back to the present. Being Nez Perce was a privilege, and she seemed to be the only person in her family who cared about that now. The bloodline that flowed through their veins defined them. Her family's history was much more than just being called Americans. Sometimes her mother acted like being Indian was a curse Nhaya slipped the necklace over her head pulling away her heavy black hair and weaving it into a braid. She examined the markings again, softly rubbing the deep etchings with her fingertips, then hid it inside her shirt. It was never meant to be in a trunk in some attic of forgotten pictures with other unimportant stuff. Her mother would never know she had found it.

Her father's death had changed a lot of things in their house, including her mother, but her mother had run away from her heritage long before that dreadful day. Closing out painful memories was not an option for her, she had no intention of doing so.

Nhaya untied the long sack that protected her bow when traveling. Her father had carved the weighty bow, made from a special hardwood, when he was only eighteen. He told her he had been given the piece of Osage orange wood from an uncle who brought it to Montana from the Great Plains. The Sioux used the wood from the hardwood trees to make their famous bows. She grasped the bow and held it proudly, as if her father was standing there watching. She stroked the single carved piece of wood, relishing its history.

She also ran her thumb and index finger up and down the string plucking it, testing its firmness. Her father's skill with that very bow had claimed the high school's archery championship four years in a row.

Nhaya planted her feet slightly apart and looked for the grip site on the bow. Carefully, she placed the arrow into its notch on the ledge below the site window. Standing tall, she brought the bow site to her eye. Her arm trembled as she struggled to draw back the string far enough to send the arrow to its target.

She missed the shot high and wide right. Wrinkling her brow in disgust, she bent over to select another arrow. How could she ever get better if she didn't practice?

"Hey!" a male voice shouted. "Don't you call out or something before you shoot? Or at least shoot in the same direction you are aiming."

Nhaya looked up from her quiver. A tall, thin, dark-haired stranger rapidly approached her through the shadows of the trees. As he came closer, she could see his bared chest heaving; her arrow clutched in his fist. Afraid, she stepped back as he closed the distance between them.

"If you were half the shot you seem to think you are, I'd be dead." He stopped short of knocking her over. His sudden closeness offended her. She immediately stiffened in defense but when she raised her face to him, she was surprised by his age. He wasn't at all the man he first appeared to be. Her fear gone, she attempted to take the arrow from his closed fist.

"I didn't know anyone was around," Nhaya politely apologized. An awkward silence hung between them. Finally, Nhaya shouted, "I said, I just didn't see you—at all."

"I know, and I'm not deaf," he barked back.

She looked at him suddenly wanting to, but resisted the motherly urge, to tuck back a lock of misbehaved hair that fell across one of his eyes, which was making it impossible for her to remain angry with him. Instead, she gently pried the arrow away from his hand and bent down to pack up her bag.

He studied the bow with interest as Nhaya scooped up her arrows and carefully placed them back into the quiver.

"Actually, I was returning here to my camp - here." He pointed.

"Oh?" Setting down her bow she looked around at the empty grounds. "You mean this is where you were camping?"

"Yeah. Why?"

"Well, to start with, I don't see any of your things here."

"Maybe I haven't brought any of my 'Things' in yet."

Nhaya held back a smirk. "Tell, me about this fire. Did you leave for a while and then return? Experienced natives know to extinguish their fires completely. This fire was never properly put out!"

His coolness to her accusation couldn't hide the sudden flamed anger in his eyes.

She didn't give him the chance to respond. "I need to go." Nhaya collected her bags and walked away.

"Next time," he called out, hold your breath before you let go of the arrow, it will help steady you. And do some push-ups to strengthen those skinny little arms of yours. That bow is made from Osage Orange, one of the hardest woods there is which makes it stiffer to pull back. That's not a bow for little girls."

That comment stopped her dead. Nhaya asked as she spun around to face him. "You were watching me?" He was gone- as quickly as he had appeared.

CHAPTER TWO

*N*haya knew she was late. The main camp area bustled with activities. The buses from Hayden and Careywood were pulling out of the camp site, their travelers delivered. The food trucks were still unloading. Chairs were being set up in the large A-framed cabin for the first service.

Nhaya passed a line of stragglers waiting to receive their week's duties and cabin assignments. Knowing she was late, she tried to slip past the camp director unnoticed, but Miss Bentley, alias "Eagle Eyes," saw her. She never missed anything. The old crone was still there.

Miss Bentley paused from her paperwork and without looking up, held up four fingers indicating Nhaya's cabin number. "It's good to see you could come back this year, Nhaya." Miss Bentley didn't bother to smile.

"Thanks. I got ya." She didn't need to be reminded of how lucky she was. For some reason, camp came a week earlier this year and on the same week of her sister's birthday. Luckily, she had saved the money and paid the camp fees early. The camp fee had been non-refundable and still her mother had tried to discourage her from going.

Nhaya chewed on a fingernail, suppressing feelings of guilt again. "Mom," she had argued, "Megan's only six." *A cake and ice cream party could wait until I get back.* Nhaya shook her head against the nagging thought. Megan would forgive her but her mother…she wasn't sure anymore.

Nhaya sprinted down the familiar path toward her new home for the week. At the fork in the trail, she stopped. A new sign pointed a different direction to the girls' cabins. The sign for the girls' cabins pointed left this year.

Nhaya passed each one, looking for number four. Every cabin looked cleaner on the outside. The broken windows had been replaced, and the doors hung properly on their hinges. She approved of the nice shade of green instead of the boring brown. The cabins were also much larger than the ones she usually stayed in, probably the reason for the exchange. More girls were coming to camp than boys.

She glanced through opened cabin's doors to welcome the newcomers. Most everyone was already settled in and getting re-acquainted. Thank heavens Miss Bentley was lenient. Nhaya was over twenty minutes late! Extra duties for being late would leave her little time for camp activities. Things were going to be different enough with Monica unable to come. As best friends, she and Monica had never missed a summer camp together. Monica was her sanity. On the other hand, Renée never missed either, but Nhaya couldn't ever get lucky enough for Renée not to show up. Renée's mother and her mother were good friends, and they were always encouraging the two of them to hang out. A blessed three weeks had gone by, and Renée hadn't called or bothered her once.

"Hey, friend, wait up!"

"Speak of the devil." Nhaya whined recognizing the irritating high-pitched voice from the trail above her. Renée must have gone to the former girls' dorms first. Ding bat. That summed up Renée. Nhaya glanced up through the trees and raised her hand to acknowledge Renée's presence.

"Oh!" Renée's voice rang out. "Love that outfit, Ny!"

Nhaya looked down. Her faded blue jeans and a white cotton shirt was not exactly an 'outfit.'

Renée looked different. Nhaya barely recognized her. She had lost weight- again. A pang of jealously rose in her. Losing weight for her seemed impossible. All Renée would do was snap her fingers and poof - she'd lose five pounds in a day!

Renée's mother was the town's hairdresser. Renée's haircuts were supposed to 'match' the times. This one reminded her of summer skunk - partially black, whips of white. She could hold back her laughter. After locating her cabin, she quickly slipped into cabin four. Nhaya held her breath and waited. "Please, please, just this time let Renée be assigned to another cabin."

After several minutes had passed and Renée didn't appear, Nhaya began to relax. She scanned the few empty beds left in the long rectangular bunkhouse. The room was almost full, and she hardly recognized half of the girls. This year many of the smaller towns from Northern Idaho had joined together for their summer camps.

Paige and Linda, who lived in Hayden, were back again. Happy to see their familiar faces, Nhaya grinned and waved.

Brenda motioned Nhaya over to her bunk. Nhaya waved. She was a Hayden regular, too. This could be Brenda last year. The age limit was eighteen and Brenda would turn eighteen at the end of next August. Nhaya wondered if Justin, Brenda's younger brother, would come back if Brenda didn't.

She and Monica, Renée and Renée's cousin, Martha, had all attended summer camp since they were young. Monica was the lucky one living in Sandpoint. It was a resort town and tourists. Lots of shopping, boating and, as Monica would put it, "and hunks!". It definitely was the place to be from. She, Renée, and Martha lived in Dover, 20 miles west in a logging town. They had all made the bus trip to Cocolalla together many times.

"Over here, Nhaya." Brenda tried to get her attention again over the noise. "I saved this bunk for you. I know you like the top." Brenda had chosen the best spot by the window and patted the one above her for Nhaya.

Nhaya's smile was genuine. "Thanks, Brenda. Sorry, my mind was on other things."

"And I saved the one across from us for Renée. I saw her earlier.

"Oh." Nhaya's face soured. She walked over to Brenda. "I have a great idea, let's not and say we tried." Nhaya laughed lightly by was sincerely hoping Brenda would get the message.

Brenda crossed her arms in front of her chest in protest to Nhaya's comment.

"Come on, Brenda, you know she's a train wreck, and everyone who gets involved with her suffers." Nhaya exaggerated a bit.

"She's not THAT bad," Brenda laughed.

Nhaya gave Brenda a 'you don't really understand' look, and Brenda responded by puckering her lips into an exaggerated pout.

"Okay, okay, you win." Nhaya's shoulders slumped. She lifted the heavy backpack and hoisted it atop her bunk.

Brenda threw her arms around Nhaya nearly knocking her over. "You're such a good sport. I've missed you!"

"Thanks." Nhaya hugged her.

"Where's Monica?" Brenda inquired.

"She's not coming at all" Nhaya replied. "She is with her father......."

"She'll be missed," Brenda smiled at Nhaya. "I can't remember a time when we didn't all hang out."

"Maybe she got a life." Paige, the dark-eyed elfin girl from Hayden, chimed in.

Everyone laughed at Paige's comment. Nhaya laughed at Paige's joke but she understood, too. Many kids were at camp because it was a safe environment for the summer. Unlike Nhaya, camp was her first choice.

"So, what have you been up to in grand Dover this summer? And how's your sister, Nhaya?" Paige asked.

Nhaya remembered she and Paige were in the same boat; both had little sisters about the same age.

"Well, let's see, the refugee camp I live in still sucks, and Megan's another year older, this week which means I'll have less hair." That comment brought laughter in the bunkhouse.

Everyone knew the saga of little sisters and finding any sort of life or hang out in Dover just didn't happen. Brenda laughed, too, and pulled Nhaya down on her bunk. Nhaya put her feet up and kicked off her shoes "Are some things better at home?" Brenda asked.

"They're okay," Nhaya said simply. Sometimes she disliked the feeling of Brenda mothering her. Brenda was two years older and probably wiser, but Nhaya didn't want to discuss things that would never change. She came to camp to get away from her problems. "So, did Justin come?" Nhaya perked up.

"Yes, he's here. So, what else have you been doing?" Brenda changed the subject. "Monica never misses camp. You said something about her father?"

"Parent problems." Nhaya replied.

Brenda waited politely for more information.

Nhaya stood up and untied her sleeping bag, rolling it out across the thin mattress above her. She really wanted Monica to be the one to tell Brenda that her parents finally split. Instead, she was vague. "Monica's dad didn't want her to come."

Nhaya placed one foot on Brenda's bed and was about to climb up when Renée made her entrance. Standing five feet seven in high heels, she stood just inside the doorway eyeing the remaining empty beds, and then her heels clicked lightly across the wooden floor to the empty bunk across from Brenda. Nhaya glanced up, not hiding her disappointment. Hopes of Renée being assigned to another cabin were short-lived.

Renée missed Nhaya's look. "Is this bed saved for someone else?" Renée asked sheepishly.

Brenda eyed Nhaya first. Nhaya kept silent so Brenda spoke up. "Guess it's yours."

Renée flashed a warm smile toward Brenda. Sitting down in her lady-like fashion, she crossed her legs at the ankle.

Nhaya mounted the bed above Brenda's. She thought about telling Renée that Monica might still show up, and she should choose another bunk, preferably at the other end of the room, but after looking down at Brenda's sober face, she kept silent.

Brenda turned over onto her stomach and tucked a pillow underneath her chin. Her tanned, slender legs crossed at mid-calf.

"Aren't those shoes a little hard to walk in up here?" Brenda asked Renée.

"Not at all. I walk in them all day long, everywhere. They are much more comfortable than tennis shoes."

Nhaya rolled her eyes at Renée's failed attempt to act high class. After adjusting her small-framed glasses, Renée looked around the room and then cleared her throat. Her words were slow and deliberate, capturing everyone's attention. "So…I guess by now everyone has heard," her excitement making her voice an octave higher.

"Heard what?" Brenda asked first, taking the bait.

Renée glanced at Nhaya before she continued. "Well, some of our very own Nez Perce community will be joining us at our camp this year." She retrieved a small piece of paper from her pocket, but before she continued, she took note of the jaw-dropping look on Nhaya's face. Renée stood up and then unfolded the paper and began to read. "Some of you know our camp's theme this year is 'Respecting Nature' and who better to teach us about Mother Nature than our very own Idaho Native Americans!"

Several girls raised their hands to clap, but Renée hushed them by raising her hand. "There's more." She giggled. "Thanks to our brilliant camp director, Miss Bentley, we will have the privilege of learning firsthand how these people lived centuries ago." After a few whistles and loud clapping, Renée took a small bow and placed the paper back in her pocket.

Nhaya sat up and unzipped her duffel bag, trying to regain some sort of composure. What had she said? "These people!?" It sounded like a side show was coming to town. She could tell Renée had rehearsed that speech! How did she know these things? It wasn't in the papers, and gossip was entertainment in a small town. She addressed Renée in an amusing voice, hoping to embarrass her. "Well, Renée, how do you think 'these people' will entertain us when they ride into town: make beaded necklaces or weave baskets out of bear grass?"

"Very funny, Nhaya." Renée's laugh sounded more like a snort. "We aren't little children."

Wanting to know more, Brenda coaxed Renée to sit next to her. Renée plopped herself down on Brenda's bunk. "They could teach us how to make dye from the juice of berries or flowers called Indian paintbrush. I also heard there will be a nature hike! Wouldn't it be killer to learn about the secret herbs and bitter roots the tribes have used for centuries? Maybe we'll mix herbs for medisipal purposes like scientists!" Renée babbled on excitedly to Brenda.

Nhaya jumped down with a thud. "Renée, the word is medicinal, M-e-d-i-c-i-n-a-l." Nhaya spelled it out. "There is no 'P'."

"So, what do you think? Cool, huh?" Renée continued.

Nhaya glanced back at Renée who seemed oblivious to her sarcasm. Renée must have missed the look again or didn't get the message because she kept on talking. "Soooo, all three of us could hang together on the nature hike." Renée pushed her wired rims up the bridge of her nose again. "With your botany knowledge, Nhaya, I'll bet we could name more specimens than anyone."

"That's species, not specimens, Renée."

"Well, that's a real good thing to know." Renée laughed, making that annoying sound again.

Nhaya rolled her eyes. "I've had it." Grabbing her jean jacket, she walked out of the cabin.

Brenda looked at Renée for an answer. Renée shrugged her shoulders. "She must be having another bad day."

From outside the cabin, Nhaya caught Renée's comment. "I'm having a bad day? I was just fine until the black plague showed up." A detour from the main path was in order. Nhaya walked away throwing her arms up in frustration. "Renée, you make me want to tear my hair out! Are you trying to make me look stupid or are you just that naïve?" Campers paused on the trail, turning to see what was causing a fight. Instead, they saw a girl standing alone waving her arms around in the air and shouting to- no one. *How did Renée know the Nez Perce community was coming to take part in the camp's activities?* Nhaya though. *It had to be her mother!* "She must have known way before and told Renée's mother." She said out loud. *So... it wasn't just missing Megan's sixth birthday that made her mother try so hard to keep her at home!*

Nhaya pulled herself up on a tree stump and kicked the caked dirt from the treads in her shoes. As mad as she was about not being told anything about the camp changes this year, she began to feel giddy with excitement. "What luck!" She had so many unanswered questions that now maybe someone could answer, like: *the markings on her necklace; what did they mean? And could someone still have a Rite of Passage after the age of thirteen? What would the Nez Perce bring to the camp? Maybe they would setup a teepee or show off their war bonnets or even wear their ceremonial headdresses.* She knew they wouldn't do the ancient ceremonial dances because they were still held sacred. She began forming a list of questions.

Tracing her father's face in her mind, Nhaya raised her hand to her own face, touching her prominent cheek bones and then moving a finger down her nose to her full lips. She didn't have his distinct features, but her skin tone and straight nose often caused people to ask about her heritage.

She considered her father's height. She had grown two inches this year. At five feet six inches she could have laid her head on his chest. She missed his frequent hugs, even his stern hand which was rarely used. It was then she would notice that the color of his eyes would change color like a spring pond after a storm. The gentle blue could turn to a murky gray when he became angry.

Like father like daughter, her mother would say. She had never noticed it.

Nhaya frowned at that thought as she worked her fingers through her hair, separating the long silky strands of black. She ran two fingers across her front teeth, remembering she hadn't brushed that day. Looking down at her cotton shirt. It was wrinkled.

She attempted to smooth it out with her hands. When she glanced up, her breath caught.

Justin was watching from a distance. Had he been watching her long? He approached in his slow but deliberate walk. "You are still a hot babe."

Nhaya dropped her hands feeling her face blush, not just because of his comment, but the foolish display of her hygiene. Just be cool, she chided herself, waiting for his advancement.

"Got any gum?" he asked.

Justin's sudden closeness made her nervous. He raised his hand toward her; she raised her hand to match his. But Justin didn't clasp her fingers. Instead, he teased her by moving his hand upward, then running his fingers through his short sun- bleached hair. She pulled her hand back and pretended to scratch her nose, her face burning with embarrassment.

"Well, do you?" His smile teased her.

"What?" She had forgotten his question.

"Gum. Do have some gum?" This time he laughed at her.

"Right." She took a deep breath and began searching her pockets and wishing she could start the conversation over again. Pulling out a piece of wrapped gum, she held it out.

"It's Double Bubble." Why couldn't it have been Dentine instead of dumb kid's gum.

This time when Justin reached for the gum, he allowed his fingers to brush across hers and linger on her fingertips. She could barely breathe as she silently watched him, stiff as a statue, unwrapped the gum. He popped the wad into his mouth and simply turned to leave. "Thanks."

"No problem," she mumbled after he was gone, her hand clutching the fingers he touched.

It was over and the spell broken. The moment she had waited for forever, and she had blown it. *"It's Double Bubble?"* Was that all she could think of to say?

Brenda walked up beside Nhaya and put her hand on Nhaya's arm. They both watched Justin strut across the grassy area to the volleyball courts. Still in shock by what just happened, Nhaya pushed herself off the stump and walked over to pick up Justin's discarded wrapper. "Littering," she attempted, but her voice came out a husky whisper. Nhaya knew she wasn't fooling anyone, but she carefully folded the gum wrapper, slipping it in her pocket. It was silly to keep it.

"It's time to give it up, Nhaya. Can't you see he's just messing with you? My brother's a ditz. You've had a crush on Justin since you were eight."

Nhaya couldn't deny it.

Brenda wrapped her arms around Nhaya. "Every time you come here; you look for a ray of hope. It's too hard to have a relationship when you only see someone one week out of the year. Besides, Nhaya, Justin isn't looking for a relationship; he's way too shallow. He has a new girlfriend every week at home."

Nhaya shrugged, pretending to not be interested in Justin's social life. "It's just that he acts like he likes me."

"Maybe he does in his own warped way. I just don't want you to get hurt. Okay? Anyway, the reason I came over here was to see what the quick cabin departure was all about?"

Nhaya had forgotten about Renée. "Renée...she just bugs me." Nhaya didn't want to talk about it.

Brenda took Nhaya's hand and led her to a grassy spot where she pulled her down to sit in the sun. "Okay, Miss Mysterious, is it because she knew about our programs for camp and you didn't?"

"Not exactly." Nhaya reached down and pulled up a piece of grass, rolling it lightly across her lips. "I was just surprised that I didn't know. My mother tried to keep me from coming to camp this year, and now I understand why."

Nhaya sat cross legged. Brenda copied her. "Ever since my father died, my mother has gone sort of nuts. She forbids me from any activities regarding our family's native traditions." Nhaya wrapped her finger around the necklace that hung beneath her shirt. "She thinks I've become"— Nhaya paused— "obsessed."

"Well, have you?"

"No! Of course not. Well, maybe a little, but that's not the point!"

"Okay. What is?"

"My father expected me to follow in his footsteps. At thirteen, he went through his Rite of Passage and earned his Indian name. I'm already sixteen."

"And your father...he tried to keep as much of your background intact as he could by taking you to the mountains and teaching you more about your heritage," Brenda chimed.

"It was our special time together."

"What does that mean, 'Rite of Passage'?" Brenda asked.

"For braves, it means becoming a man in the tribe. At thirteen, a young boy goes on a vision quest, spending the night in the forest alone and waits for his guardian spirit to reveal itself in a vision, like a bird or an animal. Then that spirit leads him and protects him the rest of his days."

"Spirits living in animals; isn't that just folklore?"

"I don't really know. All American Indian tribes have relied on animals to give them signs. The Ancients made up stories when they didn't understand how things in the universe came into being, like the sun and stars or our world. They made animals talk and gave them personalities. The Coyote is supposed to be the smartest in the animal kingdom. The ancestors made up stories about everything in nature that couldn't be explained, and they've taken great care to pass these stories on to their children and their children's children. It is still an important part of our culture."

"I would love to hear some of the stories sometime."

Nhaya gathered her thoughts. "Our history is more than that. The vision quest is a time to go somewhere away from every distraction. Being alone in the wilderness can bring a time of self-examination, a spiritual rebirth, or maybe just finding a sense of purpose."

"Is that what you are looking for?"—Brenda prodded— "some sense of purpose?"

"I don't know what I'm looking for," Nhaya said honestly. "I guess I'll know when I see it. My father also entrusted this to me." She lifted the necklace from under her shirt. "It's very old." Nhaya carefully held it out.

"Wow." Brenda examined it without touching it. "Is that part of a bone? What do these markings carved on it mean?"

"I'm not really sure. Just that my father said it belonged to a tribal shaman, and it has been passed down from the tribes before them."

"A shaman? That's a medicine woman, right? Is she magic?"

"More like knowledgeable," Nhaya said, getting pleasure out of displaying the prized necklace. "Except for Monica, Brenda, you are the only one who has seen it. My father said he would explain the markings to me, but"—Nhaya hung her head—"he's gone."

"I'm sorry, Nhaya, I can't imagine losing a parent. Do you know what I think?" Brenda asked, sitting up.

"What?"

"I think it's time you have a real boyfriend. Whatever happened to that guy who followed you everywhere at camp— the red-headed boy? He had quite the crush on you."

"Red head? You mean Adam? I wouldn't call him a red head. His hair is like a sandy blond color."

"Okay. I just remember his fair skin and freckles."

"Adam is just a friend. He left two years ago for college."

Brenda looked at her watch. "Okay. Well, I've got to catch up with Justin. I'll talk more to you at lunch."

Nhaya watched Brenda hurry toward Justin and his friends and wondered what she wanted to talk to Justin about. The lump in her throat made it hard to swallow. She brushed off her jeans, smoothed back her hair, and strolled toward the A-framed cabin.

Maybe Brenda was right, but maybe she didn't want to "give it up." Justin had come up to her, after all, not the other way around.

The weight of the necklace pulled at her neck, reminding her of its presence. Was there really a mystery to the markings on the simple piece of petrified bone? Was there no one who could tell her?

CHAPTER THREE

$\mathcal{O}$ne of the campers serving on kitchen duty rang the metal bell that hung outside the mess hall door. The clanging rang out several times before the bell fell silent, announcing lunch to the hungry campers.

Nhaya could already smell the food. Whatever they were fixing for lunch didn't have a mouthwatering appeal like fresh baked bread or the pizza she remembered eating on the first day at camp when handmade pizza used to be the tradition. Some years ago, campers had helped with creating the meals, and pizza was always one of their first choices, so it had become a staple. Back then, the pizza was something special—made with fresh ingredients and dough hand-tossed by one of the campers wanting to learn the skill. Now the pizzas came from a box, frozen and barely edible. They tasted more like the wrappers that it came in.

Nhaya didn't think twice before she rose and sprinted toward the beckoning call of the bell. There would be nothing to eat until evening, and she already felt the hunger pangs of having missed her breakfast at home. The argument with her mother before she left for camp had taken her appetite away. Nhaya worked her way toward the lunch line, cutting across the volleyball courts. Her eyes immediately picked up on Justin's location. He and Brenda were standing by the volleyball net. They seemed to be deep in conversation. Then as if on cue, both Brenda and Justin suddenly looked up and waved.

Nhaya felt the sting of betrayal. *What was Brenda telling him?* She pretended not to care that they were whispering and tactless enough to act innocent about it. Nhaya walked over and fell in line behind Paige for lunch.

Suddenly a hand caressed Nhaya's shoulder. "Brenda! You scared me," Nhaya said, pressing her hand over her heart. "I didn't hear you walk up."

Brenda smiled, keeping her hand softly on Nhaya's shoulder. "You were mumbling to yourself again."

"I was? What was I saying?" It was as if Brenda had read her thoughts.

Brenda changed the subject. "Look." Brenda secretly pointed to the front of the line where Renée and Martha stood together.

Nhaya broke into laughter. Renée had changed into a strapless red sundress patterned with large yellow daisies. Martha, at only five feet tall, stood on the stair below her, resembling a giant marshmallow. Wearing all white Martha's unusual albino skin color was equal to her naturally white bobbed hair. Both wore matching straw hats and red flip-flops. "Are they for real?" Paige turned and asked Brenda, who was still standing in back of Nhaya.

Paige smirked and lowered her voice. "How can anyone take them to be serious campers? There isn't a beach around for miles!" She glanced back at Brenda who was suppressing her laughter too. "Martha and Renée hung out together the last few weeks planning their camping attire," Nhaya, explained. "I overheard my mother talking on the phone to Renée's mom."

Martha spotted Nhaya first. She nudged Renée and both began waving wildly at her. Nhaya was aghast. She moved out of site hiding behind Paige hoping to discourage their beckoning "Maybe we should take our lunch outside today," Nhaya suggested to Brenda.

It was after one p.m. Nhaya walked a short distance from the main activities and sat down on the metal bleachers. Pulling her hair back away from her face, she slipped it into a ponytail, securing it with a hair tie from her wrist. Anticipating the first bonfire, she smiled, stirring with a sense of new excitement.

Brenda, I hope you didn't mess things up." She frowned, remembering the two whispering together.

She and Justin had not actually been a couple during camp ever, but she was a year older, and according to Monica, she was a knockout.

Nhaya looked for the new campers. The small towns of Hayden and Careywood had increased. Every year, more newcomers were showing up. Nhaya liked it better when she knew everyone. Judging by the familiar crowd she saw at lunchtime, over half of them would be paired up by the second night, sitting together at the evening campfires. Several of the regulars from Hayden hadn't made it this year, including Brenda's boyfriend, but Brenda always managed to fit in with whomever she was with.

The rays of the early afternoon sun burned hot on Nhaya's skin. Tiny beads of sweat formed across her brow. Removing her jacket, she walked over to the other side of the bleachers and sat down beneath the shade. A truck door slammed, drawing her attention to a campsite several yards across the road. Two shirtless men stood in the back of a rusty pickup, pitching boxes to a third man who stood waiting on the ground. They appeared to be setting up camp.

Grabbing her jacket, Nhaya slipped across the rutted dirt road, quietly edging her way through the trees, remaining just out of sight. Nhaya could have walked up and introduce herself. Instead, she stood back to observe them.

The first man was stocky and the shortest of the three. A beaded necklace hung on his shirtless chest. It swayed back and forth in rhythm as he lifted, turned, then tossed the boxes over the side.

The second man stood with his legs spread out. Nhaya grinned when she noticed how large the man's feet were; she guessed about size fourteen moccasins. He caught and set the boxes down easily as if they were empty cardboard.

The youngest and thinnest man of the group had his back toward Nhaya. He worked in silence, head down. She couldn't guess his age, but something about him seemed familiar. When he turned, Nhaya gasped. In her haste to remain unseen, she did not see a root of a nearby tree that protruded up from the ground. She stumbled backwards and landed hard, drawing everyone's attention to her.

The man she recognized looked at her. "Are you lost again?"

The other two stopped as well, now focusing their full attention on Nhaya. She sucked in a breath, ready to bolt when the large man wearing the moccasins dropped what was in his hands and walked over to her.

"Hello." His voice was cheerful. "I'm Light Foot." His full lips widened into a grin. He extended his strong hand to shake hers.

"Nhaya." She looked down at his large feet and managed to suppress a giggle. She reached out her hand which was instantly swallowed up in his large one.

His soft brown eyes twinkled. "Let me introduce you. I see you've met Little Snake here."

The one identified as Little Snake frowned at that comment. "And that's Mike in the truck." Light Foot pointed.

Mike nodded, putting his box down only to make eye contact.

"It's nice to meet you, Nhaya." Light Foot's voice was soft and smooth. "Damien, come over here. How do you know this young lady?"

Little Snake—Damien—jumped down from the bed of the truck. He smoothed back the same lock of misbehaved hair. "In truth, she tried to shoot me with an arrow earlier." Damien stood beside Light Foot, his arms crossed, a wry grin forming on his lips.

Was he mocking her? Nhaya scowled, furrowing her brows.

Light Foot watched as the two returned fiery looks at each other. He seemed to think they had different opinions about what had happened.

"It's a shame you missed, Nhaya," Light Foot teased.

Nhaya laughed politely, unsure of how to return the funny comment.

"Nhaya," Light Foot repeated her name. "It's native, isn't it?"

"I'm Nez Perce—one-fourth. Are you here to teach at our camp?"

Light Foot laughed. "Well, don't know if you can call it teaching, but yes, we will be at your celebration."

Nhaya searched for something else to say. She really just wanted to bolt like a deer and flee into the woods.

Mike seemed indifferent to her presence, and Damien became anything but discrete. He kept staring at her shirt. Light Foot tried to make her feel welcome in a suddenly un- comfortable situation.

"Well, it was nice to meet all of you," Nhaya addressed everyone, but her eye contact stayed on Light Foot. "I'm sure you need to get back to setting up your camp, and really, I need to get back." Nhaya turned and pointed to the road. "It's against the rules to be here," Nhaya said. That sounded so juvenile. She suddenly blushed.

"Well then walk her back to the camp, Damien, to make sure she gets back okay. I hope to see you again, Nhaya." Light Foot covered her small hand again with his. "May you travel in safety."

Damien walked cordially beside Nhaya until they were out of Light Foot's sight.

"Seems like we got off on the wrong foot," Damien suggested. "Let's start over."

It was the first nice thing he had said to her, but before Nhaya could respond, and they were out of being seen, his fingers wrapped tightly around her arm as he began to escort her across the road.

"Are you part of the ceremonies, too?" Nhaya asked him as she was being dragged along.

"Nope."

"Can you slow down just a bit? You're hurting my arm."

He let go. "Just following orders and making sure you get across the road 'in safety'."

"I can take care of myself, thank you." She shifted her shirt.

Damien looked down at her chest. "Where did you get that?" He pointed to her necklace.

Nhaya looked down wondering what he was looking at. She had forgotten to slip her necklace back inside her shirt. She quickly closed her hand over it.

Damien's attitude suddenly changed and his voice softened. "It looks old."

"It is. My father gave it to me."

"Your father. Of course. He is Nez Perce

"Yes."

"Was it handed down from your tribe?"

"I think so," she told him reluctantly. She didn't want to say too much.

"Can I please take a better look at it?"

Nhaya hesitated, but she removed her hand. "It's just a piece of jewelry." Nhaya tried to oversimplify its significance.

Damien knelt down and took the piece in his hand. "You know, this is more than incredible. I can't believe it's still intact." He took great care in turning it over in his hand rubbing his fingers lightly across the cryptic symbols like Nhaya had done many times before. She could sense his astonishment. He seemed well acquainted with the piece. She was about to ask him if he understood the encryption.

"You don't actually know what this is, do you?"

"Of course, I do." She lied, becoming offended.

"No, you really don't know. You couldn't."

"And why is that?" Nhaya became angry.

"You wouldn't even be asking that question."

One confrontation with him was enough. He was just as stubborn as he was before. "Thank you for the escort, Damien, but I really do need to get back."

He grabbed at her hand. "Look" he said, getting her attention again. "I'm sorry. It's just that…I don't know anything about you, your last name, or where you're from."

Nhaya didn't believe a bit of it. She sensed something about him she didn't like. "I'm missing archery class and somehow you seem to know how badly I need it. Maybe we'll run into each other again sometime. It seems to be my…luck." Her sarcasm was obvious.

"Well until then"—he bowed his head to her— "I'm sure we will."

"Oh, wait." Nhaya said, turning around. "One question: How did you know how I was holding my bow? You didn't come out from the woods until after I tried to shoot you."

Damien didn't answer. Once again, he had evaded her question. She watched him sprint across the road.

It was two-thirty. Time passed by quickly. She really did need to hurry. Damien—Little Snake—or whatever he went by, was exactly what she thought. He was opinionated, irritating, and rude. What made him qualified to tell her anything, especially about her father's necklace. She slipped the necklace back inside her shirt and scolded herself for wearing it.

Nhaya eyed the people hanging outside around the main cabin. Brenda was nowhere in sight. She was usually there at that time of day. Nhaya quickly took the few stairs up to the uneven planked porch. Most of the knotty pine tables and chairs that lined the porch were occupied with checker players.

She pushed the main door open and went in. The lodge, or main building, which it was called now, started out as a large one-story A-framed cabin which had been built for small church groups. The large kitchen was at the back end. Cocolalla Lodge had become a very popular place for retreats and continued to expand according to the growing needs.

Inside was like a mixture of two worlds. The older parts gave the feeling of walking into a log cabin in the woods. Smooth river rocks were brought in to build the fireplace, and a hand-carved log was set in place for the mantel. The two-story fireplace, massive in its greatness, filled one whole corner of the room. Only burned in the winters, the high piles of logs beside the hearth were begging to be used. The owners of the lodge stayed through the winters to keep all the buildings maintained; a job Nhaya would gladly accept with no pay. Nhaya pictured herself curled up in a comfy chair beside the crackling fire reading a good novel. Outside would be a winter storm, blowing drifts of snow, piling high against the windowsills.

Nhaya walked into the newer more modern portion of the lodge, passing by the long empty tables that lunch had just been served on. The smell of cleaners took the place of the earlier lunch of burgers and salads, leaving a clean scent in the air.

The newer replaced windows were a plus. It made the room much lighter inside and especially now that the room was empty. Looking at the shelves on the far wall, Nhaya could see that they had dust on them and so did the games and books. Now she wondered if anyone ever took the time to look through them. Locating the sign-up table at the back, Nhaya set her jacket down and began to thumb through the pages of classes offered.

The sign-up sheet for arts and crafts and wood carving was full. Tuesdays and Thursdays were picked this year for chess tournaments, and she noticed something new. Canoeing was a new class. Unfortunately, it was on the same day as her archery classes. She sighed and made her mark on archery, thinking about

Damien's remark. Even though she struggled to use the bow her father had made, she would never give up, regardless of her skill level.

A stirring came from the kitchen area, and she walked to the open door and peered in. Peter, sweating, walked out from the mop closet carrying a broom. He wiped his brow with his forearm and then tucked his shirt back into his jeans.

"Pete, you're on KP today?"

He held up the broom. "Good guess."

Nhaya followed him back into the newer part of the lodge and watched him tip the last metal chair on top of the long line of tables. She sat down and watched him with interest. Pete was a loner, but not by choice. He was timid and rather good looking, but his neglect for personal hygiene turned girls off. Every time she saw him, she wanted to tell him to brush his teeth more often and use a better shampoo to help the oil build- up in his greasy flattened hair.

"So, where is Monica? You two are inseparable at camp."

"Everyone has asked me that today. She's with her father."

Pete pulled a chair from the long pile of metal chairs along the wall and sat next to her. He rubbed his itching nose with the back of his hand. "Now, that I have you alone, I want to ask you something."

"Okay, shoot."

"I really care about her, you know. I have liked her - forever."

"I know, Pete," she admitted.

"It shows, huh?"

"Yeah." Nhaya stood abruptly, then strolled over to the knotty pine shelf that held the board games and puzzles. She fingered through the piles of newspapers, deciding whether to give it to him straight. Pete had as good a chance with Monica as she did in getting Justin. She decided to spare his feelings and use the tactic

Brenda used on her earlier. "Like I've been told, long distance romances don't fly."

Pete's face showed his disappointment.

"I'm sorry, Pete, I don't have the answer you want. Do you want to play some checkers?" she asked, changing the subject. "I have an hour free."

"Sure, that sounds fine."

Nhaya smiled but to her, Pete didn't sound fine at all. "I need to check the duty sheet first."

"Is this yours?" Nhaya called out, pointing to the open bag of gummy bears on a table.

"Help yourself." Pete returned an answer, He glanced outside the row of new windows. "I'll set up the board outside on the porch. I think a table just became available."

"Thanks. I'm starving!" Nhaya walked up to the bulletin board, popping a piece of candy into her mouth while searching the week's duty list, checking each page of the week. Subconsciously, she crossed her fingers and prayed that she wasn't assigned to share any duties with Renée or Martha.

I just wish you liked me less, Renée. Heaven help the person you choose to make your best friend. Luckily, none of the girls were scheduled together. She shoved the last bit of chewy candy into her mouth. She thought about Renée and her idea of hanging together all week. Someone would get an earful of her. "You will stick to them like these gummy bears are sticking to my teeth!" Nhaya blurted it out mimicking Renée's horsy laugh.

Like a cloud passing over the sun, Nhaya became suddenly aware that someone was standing behind her. In the next moment, the familiar smell of Renée's perfume confirmed the embarrassing truth. Nhaya turned and stood toe-to-toe with Renée

"W-what are you doing in here?" Nhaya's mouth dropped open.

"I saw you come in. I wanted to see what you were doing." Renée picked up the papers that had fallen out of Nhaya's hand. Nhaya fumbled for her words. "Renée, I'm really sorry you heard what I said. What I mean is I wasn't trying to make fun of you."

"At least not to my face." Renée slapped the papers back into Nhaya's hand, her eyes brimming with tears. "Who needs you for a friend anyway, Nhaya? You or your slutty friend, Monica." With that comment, Renée turned and bolted out the mess hall door.

Blown away at her remark, Nhaya hastily tacked the papers to the board and followed her out. "Why did you say that about Monica? That was totally uncalled for, Renée. Renée!

Brenda, sitting on the steps outside, watched Renée race past her with Nhaya following down the stairs after Renée. "What's wrong?" Brenda stood up. "Nhaya, where are you going?"

"Renée, come back here!" Nhaya yelled.

Without heels, Renée could run. Nhaya followed until Renée disappeared into the edge of the woods behind the lodge. Nhaya stopped, her hands on her knees, catching her breath. It was useless to continue, and at this point, she really didn't care. She turned and strode back to Brenda.

Brenda gave Nhaya a puzzled look. "What is going on between you two?"

"I hurt her feelings, I guess."

"Well, whatever happened, don't sweat it. She'll get over it."

"I just don't understand her—at all—Brenda." The two girls turned back toward the lodge, but as they did, a worried look crept across Nhaya's face as the feeling of dark foreboding settled in the pit of her stomach. This wasn't the end. It was just beginning...

CHAPTER FOUR

Flinging herself onto her bunk, Nhaya peeled off dirty socks and let them drop to the wooden floor. Having that run-in with Renée yesterday started the week off badly. She felt a little stupid now acting out her frustrations by stomping through the woods. It wasn't like her to let Renée get the best of her. She picked out a pair of worn-in jeans and her favorite soft blue, short-sleeved cotton shirt. Right now, a bath was her idea of relaxation.

Her stomach hurt. It wasn't the bacon and eggs that had given her a bellyache; it was being paired up with Renée and Brenda for the hike. Breakfast had, in fact, been peaceful, filled with anticipation of the day. Renée had acted like she didn't even know her, and that was just fine. Then, Nhaya didn't know her exciting hiking trip would be turned into four hours of having to listen to Renée expound on various subjects, in spite of the fact that, she had no knowledge of what she was talking about.

Nhaya's head was still reeling. Grabbing her towel, she jumped down and headed toward the bath houses. She felt her whole week would be ruined if she couldn't transfer to a different bunkhouse. Sitting down on the small wooden bench built into the corner of the dressing room, Nhaya could see out through the small openings in the green slatted- wood and was comforted when she knew she was alone. She quickly undressed and peeled her watch from her wrist. After wrapping herself in a towel, she shoved her soiled clothes into a travel bag and placed the sign that said "occupied" on the door. She thought twice about leaving her father's watch behind, but in all the years she had camped at Cocolalla, no one ever took stuff from the showers or dressing rooms. She thought it was mostly because no one wore expensive clothes or jewelry and never carried money. Nhaya tiptoed barefoot across the wooden walkway toward the shower stalls, avoiding the small muddy puddles.

"You're still here, Brenda?" It was more of a statement than a question. She recognized Brenda's brightly painted blue toenails and tanned feet below the steamy shower stall. "When you finish can I borrow some of your shampoo?"

"Sure." Brenda threw a small bottle of shampoo and a plastic razor over the top of her wooden door. "The hot water is running out." Brenda gave her the bad news. "It's got to be one o'clock by now. If you hurry, we can hang out before volleyball."

Nhaya caught the small bottle and plastic razor with both hands. "Thanks." She stepped into the next stall. Nhaya wound her long hair into a loose knot. It was only the second day at camp but her body already ached, and she felt like she hadn't bathed in weeks. She waited in anticipation for the first few drops to hit. When the cold water pelted her, she let out a scream of surprise. She shivered as goose flesh rose on her skin, but the briskness soon began to feel good as it cascaded over her tired achy body. The soreness seemed to wash away along with the dirt, sweat, and stress. Now she knew why she was the only one bathing. She huddled in a corner but cherished every drop.

Rubbing herself briskly with a towel, avoiding her new scrapes, Nhaya thought about Joe Eagle Feather, the person who had taught them about Nature's Medicine Cabinet on their nature hike earlier that morning. She liked him right away. He was the picture of what she thought a full-blooded Indian should be. He had such passion for what he taught, just like her father. On the nature hike, his words were carefully chosen; he only talked when there was something of importance to say, unlike some other people she knew. During their time, he was gentle in his ways and thanked the Great Spirit for making the earth and giving them the plants. He talked about more than twenty-five herbs and plants and the cures they were used for.

Then Renée would spoil everything by piping up with her pseudo intellect, asking poor Joe to repeat himself and explain things again and then asking him for the plant's "proper" name. Seriously! How could she not remember lavender, red bilberry, lemon balm, wild angelica, or sage? And if that wasn't bad enough, Renée blabbed the information again to anyone who wasn't taking notes.

Then the early morning's hike became an even bigger challenge. Nhaya had stumbled and fallen down an incline, landing on her arm and spraining her wrist. It hurt even now as she moved the razor across her leg. "How am I going to play volleyball if I can't even shave?" Nhaya's shoulders tensed again. She wrapped her hair in a towel, dried off, got dressed, grabbed her bag, and set off on the lower trail toward the lodge. Along the way, Nhaya watched the camps activities. The long-sheltered porch, surrounding the front and side of the lodge, was filled with gamers. Fans and players lined up to watch the outcome of the chess tournaments.

Nhaya recognized Pete exchanging seats with another opponent as she walked toward her cabin. Pete held up his hand indicating to her he had won the last game. She gave him a "thumbs up." Chess was not her favorite game. It took too much concentration. Volleyball was physical, and it kept her slimmer. Now she wouldn't have her edge, having to play left-handed. Nhaya gingerly moved her wrist around, checking its flexibility.

It was quiet when she entered the door of her cabin. Renée was alone sitting on her bed mumbling something to herself and scribbling in her journal. She had changed her clothes from what she was wearing earlier, and Nhaya wondered if Renée had heard the snickers about the way she was dressed. Nhaya thought about turning and leaving, but then she couldn't run every time Renée was around.

Renée said nothing to her, nothing at all, which was a bit strange, but Nhaya wasn't going to try and analyze Renée's emotions.

Nhaya yawned and opened her bag for the bottle of aspirin. She popped the cap and swallowed a couple without water.

Combing out her hair, she began to untangle the wet strands, quickly weaving her wet hair into a loose braid. Now and then she would glance down at Renée, who seemed to be totally at ease and oblivious to Nhaya's presence in the room.

It was blessedly quiet and the aspirins were beginning to work. She laid atop the bedroll across her bunk. Nhaya arched her back and stretched out, feeling it to her toes. Her eyelids were heavy and just as she was drifting off, it happened. Renée spoke.

"You don't follow rules very well, do you, Nhaya?"

Nhaya opened one eye. Renée was watching her; her pen resting in her hand.

"Pardon?"

"I saw you picking those mushrooms this morning. Did you not hear what they said about disturbing the plants and not going off the trail?"

Nhaya just looked at her, processing what she had said.

"That's obviously why you fell."

"What? Who are you now, the mushroom police?" Nhaya propped herself up on one elbow. Why did she even feel compelled to answer? "I really don't remember them saying anything about picking mushrooms." That was a lie. "Besides, I had my reasons," Nhaya said, turning her back to Renée.

"So, you're saying it is okay to not follow rules because you had your reasons." She emphasized the word "your."

"Renée, please, I'm really sorry. I think your laugh is funny, but get off my case, okay?"

Nhaya's fingers moved with stealth as she searched under her pillow for the plain brown sack where the assortment of mushrooms were stashed. After all, she had only picked a few, and she was careful not to disturb the other plants. *Why should I feel guilty over bending an unimportant rule?* She reasoned before closing her eyes. *Besides, they're not even for me; they're for Monica.*

Nhaya refused to be pushed into a false guilt trip because of Renée's or anyone else's personal problems. The little voice inside her head spoke a truth she knew: *A lie is a lie - black or white.*

Why did her conscience have to bother her now? She hummed a tune to drown out the guilty thoughts and finally drifted off to sleep, her hand still clutching the paper sack.

CHAPTER FIVE

The evening air had taken on a chill. Nhaya woke from her nap to a fly buzzing around her face. She sat up, shooing it with her hand.

Her throat was dry. She licked her lips for moisture. Through her window, she could see the sun's light growing dim, and she was angry at herself for sleeping so long.

She had the dream again, still not understanding its meaning. Most of the time her dreams were images running together that made little or no sense, which she rarely remembered. But this dream was different. Again, she could see it vividly. She checked her feet to see if they were wet or dirty.

In the dream, Nhaya ran barefoot and in slow motion across a wet grassy meadow. Then gradually, the grass became a hard red dirt path. At the end of the path stood an old woman—beautiful in her native dress. Then came the frustrating part. When the woman spoke to her, it was in a language that she had never heard. As she drew closer, the woman's wrinkled finger reached out and touched her lips. Then she understood what the woman was telling her. Nhaya hopped down from her bunk to the wooden floor and wrapped the homemade quilted blanket around her tighter. Even now, she felt the chill remembering the sound of the old woman's gentle quiet voice.

When she closed her eyes, she could almost bring back the fragrant scent of lilacs on her clothes as the woman took her hand and placed something into it. Nhaya smiled at the thought of how it had felt.

At first, the gift brought her happiness, but only for the moment. Then the weight of its responsibility turned her delight into fear. She looked at the woman.

"You must choose for yourself, my child," the old woman whispered.

"But how can I choose something that I don't understand?" Nhaya had asked. The woman took the gift away. When you are ready. She looked down. Was it the necklace?

She grasped her chest. It was still there.

Nhaya stepped barefoot outside onto the cabin's small wooden porch. It was the first time this week she had been alone in the peaceful solitude of the evening; only the crickets could be heard. She raised her face to the darkening sky, finding the evening star. It was always the largest and the first she looked for. In awe, she waited for the shiny diamonds to appear one by one that looked so close to her now. She could sit for hours at home and trace the invisible lines that brought the constellations to life. She faced east and looked intently into the sky that held the secrets to the universe. Was there really a gate to enter heaven?

The noises of laughter in the distance broke into her thoughts. The night's activities had already begun. Beyond the clearing, the first bonfire's flickering shadows rose. It was the night! The one she had waited a whole year for. Everyone would be getting reacquainted and making new friends. It was one big party. And if she was lucky, Justin might approach her again.

Slipping back inside the cabin, Nhaya grabbed her lightweight jacket from her bag, making sure to shut the door tightly to discourage forest intruders and hurried down the dark but familiar path toward the light, the laughter, and the fun.

Flames danced high into the night sky, throwing burning sparks into the air. This night would be special, now even more because of the magical feeling the Nez Perce brought to the camp. She clutched her jacket against the chill and sat down close to the bonfire, opposite of the falling ashes, and waited to be taken into their world.

The sounds of tribal drums and chanting brought goose bumps to Nhaya's arms. Several men she hadn't seen earlier in the camp across the road were dressed in full native dress with their brilliant colors and intricate designs. The men danced zealously in the orange glow of the fire, kicking up fine dust with their beaded moccasins as they moved to the rhythmic beat of the drum.

Nhaya's own heart seemed to match the rhythm, and she found herself swaying to its persuasive tempo. A sense of well-being swept over her. Perhaps it was the spirit of freedom her father had talked about. He had told her, "Nhaya, when a brave dances his dance, he dances to please his Maker, and when his Maker's pleasure is felt, there is nothing that can compare with it."

Nhaya remembered feeling that way after coming home from a church camp. Remembering the joyful songs they sang, rekindled a fire, and she felt a hint of the sweet peace again and the strong sense of belonging. That night she had given her heart to Jesus.

The music ended abruptly and the moment was over. Nhaya watched the crowd with interest. Almost everyone stood and clapped wildly, everyone but Justin. He and a girl, Nhaya hadn't seen before, sat huddled near the fire in a world of their own, his arms wrapped tightly around her as if it were freezing outside. She was oblivious to anything else but him.

Nhaya fought the pang of jealously again and quickly brushed away sudden tears. She caught Renée watching her, which was the last thing she needed—more ammo to hit her with. Lifting her arm, she hid her face with the back of her hand, as if shielding it from the heat of the fire.

It was after 9 p.m. and Nhaya scanned the crowd again, avoiding the area where Justin and his new girlfriend sat and searched for the men from across the road. Damien either hadn't seen her or didn't want to. Joe Eagle Feather was the only one sitting with the camp director.

It was then that Nhaya noticed the old woman standing alone in the back of the camp. Her shoulders were draped in a soft lavender shawl and her hand clutched a long, oddly shaped pipe. Her frame was strong and tall, not bent over by age. Her thick silvered hair was pulled back into a simple braid. Before Nhaya could see more of her, the crowd closed in between them, blocking her sight of the woman

Who was she? Only men had come to the camp from their tribe.

Nhaya rose and moved in the direction of the woman, never taking her eyes from where she stood. Nhaya had the strongest feeling she had seen this woman before. She mentally traced the lines etched in the old woman's face as she drew closer. Lazy trails of smoke rose from the woman's long pipe, surrounding her with wreaths of smoke, purple and blue shown in the low light. Nhaya was just two feet from the old woman as she pushed through the crowd. Then as if on cue, everyone around her began to move away.

The old woman stood before her and raised her walking stick as if pointing to her. Then she spoke. Nhaya couldn't understand anything the woman was saying. Then someone else called out her name. Nhaya turned to see who had called her? It was Brenda standing high on the bleachers waving over the crowd. "Come over here and sit with us." When Nhaya looked back, the old woman had disappeared. Even the odor of the pipe's smoke had faded away. Nhaya stared at the empty space where the woman had been. She remembered her trip to the coast. She had stood on the beach watching as the waves rushed to shore. When the ocean retreated, the sand was swept clean of everything that was in its path, leaving no evidence of whatever was there before. Did she just disappear into thin air?

Nhaya spotted Renée seated near the end of the bleachers; Renée was watching her! There wasn't anyone else who could have seen the woman, but she hated like blazes to ask Renée for help.

Gulping down her pride, Nhaya walked over to her. "Renée, did you see where the Indian woman went that I was talking to a minute ago?"

"What woman?" Ignoring her question, Renée emptied the rest the popcorn in her mouth and began chewing it loudly.

"What do you mean, 'what woman'?" Nhaya took the empty box from her hand, then stared her in the face. "The old Indian woman I was just standing close to—right over there." Nhaya pointed. "You know you were watching me."

"You weren't with anyone but yourself. You should really lay off the mushrooms, Nhaya. How about some more gummy bears, instead?" Renée's voice mocked her.

Nhaya winced. "Okay, fine. I understand this game." Nhaya walked away.

"You are not my friend anymore," Renée called out!

Again, Renée had made her feel like a fool. Renée had a way of getting her to react. Nhaya knew she shouldn't have walked out on their conversation that first morning. Whether Renée's bragging about knowing the revised camp's activities was just to bug her or intended to make her look more important, Nhaya knew she needed to react less. Asking to be transferred to another cabin would be her loss, not Renée's.

Nhaya checked her watch. It was almost 10 p.m. curfew. No wonder she felt rotten. She hadn't eaten since morning. If she hurried, she could still make the canteen. It would close in ten minutes. She made a beeline to the lodge.

Standing at the empty counter, she opened her wallet and pulled out five dollars. "Can I have three of those candy bars"— she pointed to the Snicker bars—"and a bag of buttered popcorn, please." Then she remembered Justin's earlier remark, "Still hot." Hopeful, she put the five back in her wallet and pulled out a dollar bill instead. "Umm, never mind. Just give me a large water and a small bag of unbuttered popcorn, please."

CHAPTER SIX

$\mathcal{N}$haya reached the lodge, her breath labored as she sprinted up the rest of the steps, a piece of paper clutched in her hand. She stopped in front of Brenda.

"I've been called to the counselor's office!"—she suddenly lowered her voice realizing she was gaining unwanted attention and finished the sentence in a forced whisper—"this afternoon. Do you know anything about this?"

Brenda closed her book and turned her attention to Nhaya. "No, I don't," she said in innocence. "It's only Wednesday and you are already in trouble?" Brenda made a joke and offered Nhaya a sip of her orange soda. "Sit."

Obediently, Nhaya took the bottle and sat herself down in the wooden rocking chair next to Brenda. "I am at a total loss. I get this slip of paper"— Nhaya waved it—"off my bed and no one sees anything. It must have been put there at lunchtime." Nhaya handed it to Brenda. "Oh, Brenda offered. It must be one of those pranks."

Brenda read the complaint. "It looks real. It says you are supposed to be in the counselor's office in ten minutes. Are you going to go?"

"I hate to bring this to you." Nhaya said embarrassed, her voice almost a quiver. "You know, Monica couldn't come this year; she has always been here to give me good advice. What do you think What should I do?"

"Can you give me any idea……?" Who filed a complaint on you?

They don't give you much to go on here?" They both scanned the note together.

"Does this have something to do with Renée?" Brenda coaxed her to spill.

Nhaya looked sheepish. "I had a bad moment." "A bad moment?"

Nhaya cringed. "I'll tell you about it later."

"My advice: Go and don't be late."

Nhaya didn't want to believe it. Would Renée really stoop this low? This was a private problem between the two of them, not part of the camp. She had hoped Brenda would agree that it was just the usual prank.

She pressed Brenda again. "Remember two years ago, Brenda, all the socks suddenly disappeared from every girl's dorm, and they were found later heaped up in a pile by the boy's bathrooms."

Brenda nodded her head in agreement. "And after that, it was bras." Brenda laughed.

Nhaya remembered poor Ginny. After the sock ordeal, Ginny's brother, Sam, thought it would be funny to take his sister's bras, pass them around, and wear them as bonnets. "Boy did Sam get into trouble. Sam swore it wasn't his idea. Because he was younger, the counselors decided someone else had instigated it. Still, his mother was called." Nhaya crossed her arms, gripping her shoulders, feeling the embarrassment of it all. "I can't have my mother called Brenda. I will never get to come back to camp -EVER!"

Brenda held the note up and looked at it again. "This isn't like that, I'm sure," she reassured her.

Nhaya stood and reluctantly reached out to take the paper. A kid from behind them batted it out of Brenda's hand and was backing up to run.

"Give me that!" Brenda snapped at him.

Justin came up from behind the boy and snatched the wrinkled paper from his hand. "Bill, you are a twit." He slapped Bill on the side of his head and handed the note back to Nhaya.

"Sorry, Nhaya." Justin apologized for Bill.

"Thanks." Nhaya felt too embarrassed to meet his gaze.

Nhaya began her walk down the narrow trail to the counselor's office, her head down. With every step, she became more concerned that it was Renée who was involved.

It was exactly one minute after two when Nhaya stepped through the counselor/first aid's cabin door. Miss Jenkins wasn't there. Her nose wrinkled up at an unpleasant odor coming through the opened office door. It came from a half- eaten egg sandwich left on Miss Jenkins's desk that was warming in the afternoon sun.

Taking a large leather-bound dictionary set between the few select books on the shelf, Nhaya picked it up and slumped down in a nearby chair. She flipped the pages of the heavy book, finding the word "disgruntled" That was the charge against her. The dictionary described the word to mean displeased, angered, or dissatisfied, etc. That sounded about the way she felt. But taking someone's property wasn't a crime.

After Renée's conversation with her regarding protocol and rules of conduct, Nhaya believed that Renée had done just that—stolen. She reasoned it was none of Renée's business if she left the trails or picked a few extraordinary specimens of mushrooms to take home for Monica. Her well-chosen picked and cleaned mushrooms had simply vanished. There was no one else to blame but her.

Something dropped on the open windowsill interrupting another one of Nhaya's self-talks. Nhaya stood very still as a large black bird stretched out its wings, revealing its stocky white underbelly. This was not just any bird; it was a hawk. When the regal hunter dipped its small head, the stubby brick-red tail feathers rose into view, telling her the exact species: a red- tailed hawk. The large bird seemed unconcerned with her presence and moved in closer, eyeing the scraps of smelly sandwich left on the paper plate. Then, dropping something from its hooked beak, the bird exchanged whatever it was for what was left of the sandwich.

"What do you have?" Nhaya walked carefully toward it. She jumped back at the bird's screech and sudden flapping of its powerful wings.

"Dumb birds," her confidence shot. "I don't care if you want That stupid sandwich!" Composed, Nhaya walked over to the desk. She should have remembered that hawks were vicious predators. It could have attack her.

At first glance, Nhaya thought the round object dropped by the bird was a bottle cap. Stepping closer, she picked it up along with a few blades of grass. She put her finger through the center of the caked dirt and gasped. Holding her hand up, she slipped the large ring onto her finger.

Nhaya looked at the time. Miss Jenkins was late. Taking it off again, she pushed it deep into her pocket, deciding to examine it later.

Since she was in the counselor's office, Nhaya decided to ask about the mysterious woman that Renée did not seem to notice at the bonfire the night before. All the staff would know who attended. The campgrounds couldn't be totally secured, but everyone kept a close watch on anyone or anything that looked out of place.

Nhaya groaned with boredom, gazing longingly outside the window at the volleyball game about to start. She would miss her archery lesson, too, if Miss Jenkins didn't show up soon. *"Adults. why did they get to show up late?"*

Brenda had just returned a volley. It hit the top of the net and bounced back. If she was playing center front, she could have saved that shot! Nhaya walked back to her chair and dropped into the seat with a thud.

Nhaya thought about Renée's accusation against her. Guilty as charged. She rubbed at her face. It was true, she always reacted before she thought, a bad flaw in her character. She relived the scene. When she had discovered the mushrooms were gone from under her pillow, her anger had hit. "Okay," she had shouted, already assuming it was her. "Where are they?" She immediately dashed over to Renée's bed in front of everyone and began rummaging through her stuff. Renée just stood there, horrified. Then she accused Renée of being a thief. The search turned up empty. She just knew it was her. Case closed.

At that point, Miss Jenkins, a tall slender woman dressed in a crisp white buttoned-down cotton shirt and knee-length safari shorts, entered the room. She quickly motioned with her hand for Nhaya to stay seated. "Sorry, Nhaya, for being late."

"Hello, Miss Jenkins." Nhaya looked up, trying to read the emotion in the woman's face that was partially hidden under her green plastic visor.

Miss Jenkins got to the point. "I've received some disturbing news from one of your bunkmates, Nhaya. Do you want to tell me your side of this story?" Miss Jenkins began moving about the room. She seemed a bit disturbed.

Nhaya sighed resigned, "I don't really have a side," How could she possibly prove it any way. The evidence was gone.

"Then you have no defense for your actions?" She looked directly at Nhaya, her face neither angry nor surprised.

"No, ma'am." Nhaya wanted to spill her guts- tell her why she went ballistic. Instead, she lowered her eyes. "You have never been in detention before, and you've been coming to this camp for a long time, Nhaya."

What's troubling you?" Nhaya was taken back by Miss Jenkins' sudden display of compassion. She decided to ask the burning question that was driving her nuts. "Are there any other Nez Perce joining us, other than the five men?" Nhaya paused. "Like an older woman?"

Miss Jenkins looked puzzled. "No, I don't think so, why? Does this have something to do with you and Renée?"

"No, I just wanted to ask. May I leave now?" Nhaya glanced at her watch. "I have archery in twenty minutes."

Miss Jenkins rubbed her fingers across her forehead. "You know, I can't just dismiss this without some recourse, Nhaya. Since we are halfway through the week, I won't call your mother. Nhaya looked up, relief on her face.

"Nhaya, I am sorry but you don't seem to show any remorse for your actions. That's what concerns me more."

"But I didn't do anything that warrants punishment, Miss Jenkins. This was between me and Renée, personally. It's over."

Miss Jenkins looked thoughtful. She wrote something in her book while Nhaya held her breath.

"I'm putting you on KP, including mopping floors and garbage detail every night for the duration of the camp."

"Every night?!" Nhaya's face became flushed. "Don't you think that's a little harsh? I'll miss everything!"

"I'm sorry, Nhaya. Unless you have anything else to tell me, you may go." The counselor's book closed with a thud.

Nhaya rose. "No, you aren't," she whispered to herself as she closed the door behind her. Nhaya walked back to the bunkhouse to grab her bow. At least she didn't run and squeal to the camp director. Renée had violated the unwritten law at camp: WHAT HAPPENS IN THE CABIN STAYS IN THE CABIN. If everyone who had issues took them up with the camp superintendent, there would be no camp. If there was a good side to this, it was that her mother wouldn't have to drive up. That was the worst possible thing that could happen. There were only three nights left. Maybe she could get off for good behavior.

Nhaya spotted Renée sitting alone on the cabin doorstep. Her anger burned again as she picked up the pace and stormed towards her. Renée immediately stood up, tripping over her own feet as she backed into the cabin.

Nhaya's advance was quick. Renée reached her bed, grabbed her diary from underneath her pillow and wrapped it tightly in her arms. She tried to get out of the room by skirting around to the open door, but Nhaya anticipated the move and blocked it.

Renée stopped, and suddenly stood tall, her voice bold. "I didn't touch your stupid mushrooms!"

"Right now. I don't care about them. You've just ruined the rest of camp for me!"

Renée advanced again, claiming the right to leave. Nhaya's stance was solid, waiting for battle. Renée brushed past her, but Nhaya pushed her back with more force than she had intended. Renée reeled backwards colliding with the edge of a bunk. As she fell, her glasses flew off her face. Renée got to her knees and began searching for the fallen spectacles.

"It was bad enough that you refused to help me last night,"—Nhaya pointed a shaking finger at her—"but being a tattletale and taking things that don't belong to you is going to cost you, believe me. How would you like me to remind everyone about the lies you spread about Monica last year being pregnant? Maybe you have forgotten them but I haven't!"

Renée retrieved her glasses from under Brenda's bunk. She sat down and rubbed the lenses with her shirt. Her hands were shaking.

"Look, Nhaya, we really got off on the wrong foot this year," she said in a softer tone. "I-I don't want World War III. I didn't see any Indian women last night, honest." Her voice was hushed. "And I really don't care if you picked those stupid mushrooms. Like you said, it wasn't any of my business."

Nhaya gawked at Renée. How could she turn around so fast and sound- so convincing? But lying seemed to be easier than admitting you were wrong. She was learning that and there always seemed to come back and bite.

Renée sat rigid, her hands cupped around the edge of the bed railing, watching for an opportunity to escape.

Nhaya's anger dissolved. What was done was done. What more could she do to Renée? Nhaya glanced out the door. Several of their bunkmates were coming down the path.

"Hey, maybe someone is playing a joke on you," Renée spoke up. "Or-maybe the house mother found the mushrooms and threw them away." Renée's voice became even more convincing. "I'll even help you look for them if you like."

"No." Nhaya held her hand out in protest.

"Truce?" Renée offered her hand.

Nhaya retreated outside. Renée just didn't get it. The mushrooms weren't the only reason for her angry outburst. Because of Renée, she would miss the best part of camp—the evenings; sitting at the campfires, perhaps another chance with Justin, and the hopes of seeing the old woman again. Nhaya let out a heavy sigh. She suddenly felt drained.

CHAPTER SEVEN

*I*t was Saturday morning. What had been a year of waiting—counting the months and the weeks—was over. And like every camp week, there would be memories to tuck away. The morning sunlight streamed ribbons of gold through the window above Nhaya's head. She crossed her legs and sat on the stripped-down mattress; her head bent low. Nhaya pretended not to pay attention to the cheerful goodbyes or observe the hugs and well wishes among friends. The anger over her punishment had been replaced by the insidious feeling of self-pity.

No one seemed to even notice that she wasn't around for the evening activities, except Brenda. Nhaya flinched at the chirps of the golden meadowlarks who seemed oblivious to her pain.

Renée had already packed her bags and left, probably to avoid another confrontation. She had stayed clear of her after their second run-in.

An odd thing had happened late one night. while she was working off her kitchen detention that she could not explain. She was busy taking out the trash. She heard a rustling sound. The same hawk was sitting on top one of the trashes can lids behind the kitchen. It refused to move even when the back kitchen screen door shut. She stood for a moment hoping it would fly away. It just sat there and stared. She flapped her arms up and down to scare it away, then she tried talking to it. "Do you want the ring back?"

She had laughed. Finally, she edged closer raising the trash bag in her hand, The stubborn hawk moved to a tree limb but didn't fly far. It continued to squawk at her then flew away.

The night was unusually quiet; not even the laughter that typically came from the dorms was there. She remembered beginning to feel nervous, because the hawk seemed to be staring at her, following her every move. She heard a rustle and peered into the forest, which she had never feared now became dark and foreboding as if someone was lurking in the darkness watching her, too.

Hurried, to dump her trash, she opened the lid and there on top was her sack of mushrooms. Nhaya looked around in disbelief. Had they been left there for her to find? Was Renée hanging back watching her? She took them back inside but decided not to mention it to anyone. Had Renée discarded them, or had it been the den mother, after all?

Nhaya's fingers clutched the box and she stuffed it deeper into her duffle bag along with her soiled clothes.

When someone called out her name as they were leaving the cabin, Nhaya looked up and acknowledged them. Dropping her sleeping bag to the floor, she checked one last time under the lumpy mattress for misplaced socks.

"You were staring in a daze, Nhaya. Are you Okay?" Benda asked.

"Yeah, I'm okay."

"Well, my mom is coming to pick me up. I might not see you next summer." Brenda leaned against Nhaya's bed.

"Lucky you. Say hello to her and tell your boyfriend he missed a great week." Nhaya's voice was bitter. She hadn't caught Brenda's comment about not coming back. She threw her last bag down.

Brenda gave her a sad look. "Don't be so gloomy. I can't figure out what you see in Justin, anyway. He isn't even your type."

"What did you tell your brother about me?" Nhaya figured Brenda had discouraged him.

"I didn't say anything about you, Nhaya. That day by the net, I was asking him about Tom and why he didn't make it. I keep away from Justin here. I have to put up with him and his attitude at home but not here."

"Oh." Nhaya gave Brenda a weak smile. "So, who is my type?" Nhaya jumped down and sat on Brenda's bed.

"Just someone more like you, I guess."

"And what does that mean?" Nhaya began to feel defensive. Brenda sat down next to her. "Well, for starters, someone who was born with a brain and someone who doesn't think he's the only person on the planet." A serious look replaced Brenda's smile. "Just find someone with good values, someone who is really into you."

"You really think Justin's all that bad?" Nhaya said, defending him. "He's your brother."

"Yes, he is and I know him he's a selfish brat. You need a hero and he's not one. They're out there somewhere; you just haven't found him yet."

"Well, while you are helping me look for these 'heroes,' can I add good looking to the list of wants?" Nhaya held a pretend pen and paper in her hand as if writing her list. "Let's see."

"Yes, let's not forget a great bod and tight abs." Brenda took a mental picture of Tom.

Nhaya thought of Justin and his tall skinny build. It didn't matter to her if he was buff. His large placid blue eyes could melt anyone.

Brenda noticed the tears forming in Nhaya's eyes. "Hey, this was supposed to be fun."

"It's just been a bad couple of days," Nhaya said as she brushed tears from her face.

"I'm sorry about Renée, too." Brenda stroked Nhaya's hair. "You were right. She can really be a pain."

"Now you notice." Nhaya poked fun at Brenda. She wiped her tears, but this time they were accompanied with laughter. "I have been such an idiot, Brenda. I have been so self-consumed. You were missing Tom all week, too."

"I'll see him back in Hayden tomorrow. Monica didn't come to camp either and I know you missed her tons. Next year will be better for you." Brenda reached out and gave Nhaya a high five.

"Hope to see you next year." Nhaya smiled as she watched her friend disappear into the group of remaining girls that were waiting to board their buses. She had a feeling camp days would never be the same. Nhaya waved, although she knew Brenda didn't see her.

Nhaya stood by herself in the quietness of the bunkhouse wanting to linger a little longer. After giving the strings of her bag a final tug, she propped it up against the door and stood with her arms crossed. With a wistful sigh, Nhaya stared past the path to the sturdy tall pines that would still be there next year and the year after that. She could always rely on nature; green forests, the returning of spring with its renewed beauty, skies that, no matter where she traveled, would always show off their wonders. So had it been with her father's love - constant and reliable. Now, she wondered who her champion would be. She needed so much more than a handsome face. Brenda was right. Beside Justin's obvious good looks and hypnotic eyes, what else did she see in him? She really couldn't answer that question. She did need a hero. But would she ever find him?

Nhaya was almost the last one to board. The driver seemed to remember her and gave her a look as she jetted up the steps finding the same seat she sat in on the journey up. She avoided the bus driver's eyes in the mirror watching her as she contemplated opening the window then deciding against it. Pulling a magazine from her backpack instead, she kicked off her tennis shoes and settled in for the hot three-hour ride.

Luckily, the trip never seemed to take as long going back. She was sure her mother would be waiting for her and with all kinds of questions. Boy, could she tell her a few stories.

Mom will pop her cork if I tell her the half of it, especially about almost getting kicked out of camp.

Exhausted, Nhaya turned a page in the magazine without looking at it. Life, for her, had turned a page, too.

A few minutes had passed when she remembered the ring and searched her pockets. Wiping off the rest of the dirt, her curiosity peaked when she discovered something had been crudely etched inside. It resembled a pair of roughly carved wings She held it up. *Where did the bird get this ring?*

The last bit of her free time had been spent questioning everyone about the mystery woman. No one had seen her. Were they all blind? *I am not crazy, she was there.* She certainly stood out in her beautiful array of colorful garments, not to mention the unusual pipe and large carved walking stick. She looked like she just stepped off the cover of a *National Geographic* magazine.

Throughout the bus, heads were nodding off to sleep. Nhaya looked over her shoulder. Legs hung over the side of the seats with shoes discarded. Renée was sitting in the very back seat looking out the window. Martha sat beside Renée; her nose buried in a book. Nhaya couldn't see the title. Nhaya ran a finger across the top of her chapped hands. If she ever washed another pot or pan it would be too soon.

She thought about Damien. He was totally different than anyone she knew— older, mysterious. He was clearly stuck on himself but sort of in a charming way. *What happened to him?* A thought hit her. He wasn't part of the celebration, and he wasn't staying at the campgrounds, so why was he helping Light Foot and Mike set up their camp? Maybe he was there for… She had no idea, and it was highly unlikely their paths would ever cross again. In a way, she hoped so, and then again, she didn't.

As the bus made its turn from the Cocolalla campgrounds onto highway 95, Nhaya stared out the dust-covered window, listening to the blur of passing summer vehicles, uninterested and unaware of her surroundings.

It was Nhaya's usual custom to turn around and say farewell to another incredible week at camp, but this time her heart just wasn't in it.

Had she turned just once, perhaps she would have noticed the young dark-haired man standing along the roadside. She would have also seen him watching carefully to determine which direction the bus was headed. But instead, Nhaya was lost in a memory of the few moments shared with Justin.

CHAPTER EIGHT

*T*ime flew by unnoticed. Nhaya was close to Sandpoint already. Her favorite part of the trip was coming up. She could see the beginning of Long Bridge which crossed over part of the Pend Oreille River. The bridge was once the largest wooden bridge in the world. Its well-worn planks made a soothing, rhythmic sound as the tires rolled across each section. They seemed to be saying in rhythm, welcome back Nhaya, welcome home…welcome.

Nhaya gathered her things, preparing to get off the bus. Dover was only twenty minutes from Sandpoint. Surprised, she was actually excited to get home. Not that she was becoming paranoid, but she reached down into her backpack just to check. The small, double-wrapped box was tucked securely away. *It would be fun giving Monica the mushrooms along with telling her the crazy story of their survival.*

The gentle rocking of the bus was comforting. She laid her head back, closed her eyes and waited. The bus had already rolled across the final section of Long Bridge, and the fingers of the lake's tributaries were passing out of view. The mountains, most of the trees, and the thick undergrowth, had disappeared. Now the landscape was filled with blue wild rye and June grass. Only a few minutes more and they would be at the station. Her mother and Megan would be there waiting for her. She would be glad to see them both

———∞∘)◯(∘∞———

The Sandpoint bus terminal looked small and old-fashioned from the outside, but inside was surprisingly spacious and modern. Nhaya had been prepared to be one of the first one off. Inside the station, she moved quickly through the travelers, looking for Megan. Someone grabbed her arm and turned her around.

"I thought that was you!"

"Adam? You're back in town?" Nhaya dropped her bags and reached up for a hug. "Oh, my gosh, you've changed. I hardly recognized you." Adam's easy grin gave Nhaya a familiar feeling of comfort. She had forgotten their closeness and how often she had relied on him.

"Yeah, I might have changed some. It's been a while since I've been home."

"It's been over a year. The last time we were together, you were getting ready to leave for England."

"It's been almost two years," Adam recounted.

Nhaya touched his arms. "I just can't get over how different you look; you're so - grown up!" The few remaining freckles on Adam's cheeks began to redden.

"Looks like you've been gone awhile yourself." Adam looked down at her various bags.

"Just a week...at camp." Nhaya laughed, looking down, feeling a little embarrassed. Camping gear for her used to consist of a pair of shoes, a change of clothes, and a toothbrush.

"Well, how was it this year? You've always been a real die- hard for the woods."

Nhaya looked up, surprised by his remembering such a small detail about her. "Oh, it was great as always. Why are you here at the bus station? Are you leaving town again?"

"Nope, I'm here for good. I just got this part-time job a couple of days ago. I'll be working here until college starts up again. So, since it's my job to help the passengers, let me." Adam gave her a quick wink.

"Thanks. You can take my sleeping bag. My arm's killing me."

He lifted it with ease, grabbing her bag as well. "You've grown taller yourself," Adam remarked, looking her up and down.

"Really?" Embarrassed by her grunginess, Nhaya straightened the shirt she had worn two days in a row and stood a little taller. She flipped back her hair, running her fingers through it. A shower was never part of her last day of camp activities knowing she would be sweaty from the ride home. She wanted to wait in anticipation of a luxurious bubble bath in her footed tub to scrub off the week's grime.

"Is someone picking you up?" Adam asked as they walked through the double doors toward the parking lot.

"Well, I thought my mom would be here." Nhaya kept looking around.

"If you need a lift, I'll be off in about fifteen minutes." Adam set her things down in front of a wooden bench and tucked in his white work shirt.

"Thanks, Adam…" Nhaya's voice trailed off. "I am really glad you're back."

Nhaya watched him as he disappeared back through the doors. She looked at the hands of her father's watch and tapped the glass. They were still moving. It was two o'clock. "Where are they?"

Nhaya removed her backpack and stepped into the telephone booth at the corner of the building. She reached into her jeans pocket and produced enough change for a call. The familiar voice answered.

"Mom, you're still home? I'm back. The bus just pulled in. You're picking me up, right?"

"Oh…of course. Time has just slipped away from me," Miriam said.

"Oh…that's okay." Nhaya tried to make her answer sound casual.

The line was silent.

"Umm, I can ride home with Adam if you're too busy," Nhaya said. She suppressed her hurt.

"He's there at the station? I didn't know Adam was home."

"Yeah, and he looks so great, Mom. He's grown about two feet."

"He has a car?"

"I guess so. He offered to give me a ride."

"Well, make sure you come straight home. Megan is driving me crazy wanting to see you."

"Okay. Love you." She waited but her mother had already hung up. "Bye…" Nhaya stared at the receiver in her hand then lowered her head. *I guess I wasn't important enough for you to remember to come and get me.* Nhaya's mind couldn't understand the why, but her heart did. She hung up the phone.

"So, you need a lift?" Adam was standing beside her. "That was a short fifteen minutes," Nhaya said.

"They let me go early. Is it okay with your mother if I drive you home?"

"She doesn't care."

"You still live in the same place?" Nhaya nodded.

Adam grabbed her suitcase and swung the sleeping bag over his shoulder.

They walked together in silence across the parking lot. Then Adam stepped ahead of her near the last row of parked cars.

"I park back here, less likely to get a dent." He stood in front of a 1963 white MG convertible.

"Holy cow!" Her jaw dropped. "This is your car? It's - incredible!" Nhaya ran her fingers across the highly polished finish.

"It's used." Adam followed behind Nhaya, his hands re- tracing her fingertips on the smooth finish. "I bought it from a guy who was moving to Alaska last summer. I wouldn't want to ride around up there in Alaska in this baby either." Adam unlatched the ragtop and folded it down into its compartment. "May I?" He opened the passenger door and bowed low.

"You may." Nhaya couldn't suppress a giggle. She threw back her hair in theatrical style. "You still know how to make me laugh." She began to feel better. Things hadn't changed between them, even after two years.

The air seemed unusually humid for Northern Idaho. As she fanned herself, she took note of the billowing clouds building in the distance and wondered if a storm was coming. She started to feel uneasy and anxious again, like she had over the past week. Even the warm summer nights had taken on a chill. She shivered just thinking of what happened at the back of the kitchen. She was sure someone was watching her when she found the mushrooms. After that night she felt someone was watching her. The entire week had started out bad. She wasn't going to let it happen to her again.

The parking lot pavement was hot, and the car smelled of fresh wax. Nhaya slid into the car and sat waiting. It was Adam's funny laugh she remembered most as he hopped in next to her and turned the key. The motor had a deep rumble like a dragster ready to race.

Adam put his arm across the back of Nhaya's seat as he backed out between the maze of parked cars. Nhaya noticed the envious stares of the people who turned to gawk.

"Maybe I'll let you drive it sometime," Adam said, teasing her. "I'd love to!" She didn't want to tell him she didn't even have her driver's permit yet.

Once inside, the car smelled of new leather. Adam kept everything perfect. Nhaya lightly ran her hand across the textured seat. It still felt cool to her touch. She had never been in such a low-seated car before. *Monica was going to flip her lid.*

"Hold on to your hat!" Adam shifted into gear. He raced the car across the parking lot onto the two-way street.

The sun burned hot on Nhaya's face until the car picked up more speed. Nhaya shaded her eyes with her hand wishing she had actually brought a hat. She caught the glimpse of a large bird perched high on a telephone wire. She turned in her seat to get a better look." It just can't be!".

"What are you looking at?" Adam asked.

She pulled stray hairs away that whipped her face by the wind and sat back in her seat. "I was just looking at a bird on that wire."

"Well, while you are doing nothing, put your seat belt on. I don't want to lose you going around some corner," Adam scolded.

"You sound like my mother." She settled into her seat.

Nhaya glanced over at Adam behind the wheel and thought about Justin. If he could see her now, he might see her differently. After all, Adam was older and he had a car and not just some heap, either. But that would never happen and Nhaya knew it. She looked over at Adam; he seemed to be reading her mind. She gave him a sweet smile. He laughed his contagious laugh and Nhaya decided Justin was way below her ideal hero.

"How have you been?" Adam called out over the noise of the wind and roar of the engine.

"Fine. How about you?" She could barely hear her own voice.

"Great, now that I'm back."

"You didn't like Europe?"

"I just prefer living here." Adam gave her another warm smile. The car stopped at the train tracks.

"I would love to have the chance to go somewhere exciting," Nhaya said. "Maybe live with my aunt in Montana. I've thought about maybe doing that next summer. What do you think?"

"If that's what you want to do." He shrugged. He grinned and shifted into first gear and slowly moved over the uneven tracks.

For some reason, his answer didn't satisfy her. She was hoping for a longer discussion…that he would try and talk her out of it.

"Did you get contacts?" Nhaya decided to change the subject. "Yeah, before I left for England." More silence.

Despite her efforts, she found it hard to keep the conversation going. Before Adam left, they had talked a mile a minute about anything and everything. Maybe she had done all the talking, and he had done all the listening. But there had never been an unnatural silence between them. Now Adam seemed different, more mature. She fingered the leather strings on her soft beaded belt, occasionally looking over at him. Adam kept his eyes focused on the road and appeared comfortable with the silence.

Her eyes moved across his chest. His well-shaped arms were stretched out over the steering wheel. He had definitely filled out. The t-shirts he used to wear were loose fitting. Now they hugged his body, revealing muscles she hadn't remembered. She thought about Justin standing next to her at camp. He was pencil thin. Conscious that she had been staring at Adam since she had gotten into the car, she forced herself to concentrate on the scenery outside.

Then, without warning, the car leaped after hitting a bump and Nhaya found herself floating above the seat, restrained by the belt. She landed with a thump and her breath rushed out between pursed lips. She grabbed a hold of the dashboard and stared wide-eyed at Adam. He was laughing hysterically.

The tires hugged the winding country road like they were made for the speed. Nhaya held fast to the dashboard, her feet planted firmly on the floor. When Adam finally brought the MG to a short stop at the turnoff to Dover, she gave an audible sigh.

"You don't like fast cars?" Adam removed his sunglasses to look at her.

She ignored the question. Her skin felt tight from the wind and the heat of the afternoon sun. She smoothed her hair down, wishing she had braided it. Adam's sandy blond hair, on the other hand, never moved.

She hadn't noticed it until then but she realized Adam was trying to impress her. Brenda's advice came to mind: Find someone who was interested in her. Time had changed Adam. She realized he was flirting with her.

"Do you want to go to the lake later this afternoon and play some volleyball?" she decided to ask. "Everybody should still be hanging out there. They will all be glad to see you."

"Sure, I could bump a few balls around; it's not too late in the day. I'm off work until tonight."

"I'll see if my mom will take us and bring us back."

"Nhaya, I have a car."

"Oh, right" *That was really dumb.*

"How about I give you an hour or so. You can unpack all those bags." Adam laughed.

"I can just change." She punched him in the arm.

"Then it's a date."

"A date?" Nhaya asked.

"Sure, you know what a date is, don't you? Guy picks up girl and they go out?"

"Very funny." Nhaya blushed again.

Adam slowed the car to a sensible speed. Nhaya mentally began to whittle down her 'to do' list for the day. Laundry, washing her hair, and hanging out with Megan could wait until tomorrow. Monica had her father's car. They could shop for Megan's birthday present. Maybe even take Megan with them. Pleased with her plans, she sat back in the soft leather seat, tightened her seatbelt, and watched the ribbon of highway rise and fall beneath the wheels of the very fast car.

CHAPTER NINE

$\mathscr{A}$dam turned down the familiar road he had walked many times before with Nhaya. Now he pulled the MG over to the curb in front of the only occupied house left on the block. He revved the motor twice before turning it off. In one swift motion, Adam cleared the steering wheel with his long legs and stepped over the short door without opening it. Before Nhaya could process his shocking exit, he was standing next to her. He offered her a hand.

"I hope you don't think I'm getting out the way you just did?"

Suddenly she was suspended in mid-air. Adam had reached in and lifted her out of her seat as easily as if she'd been a doll. He put her down gently on the grass.

"Very funny, Adam." Nhaya tried to regain her dignity.

"I brought you home in one piece, didn't I? I was just trying to provide you with great service, too."

Adam looked at their large front yard. The grass needed cutting and the trees were matured and overgrown. It was too much for a woman and two kids to keep up. He could see part of the old barn and the garage behind the house. Every building needed a good cleaning and a couple of coats of paint. "Well, the house hasn't changed," Adam remarked. "Same color blue, same white shutters. Even the porch swing is overflowing with your stuffed animals."

"You goof, they're Megan's."

"Could have fooled me," he teased her. "I seem to remember that long-tailed monkey over there, the one missing an arm."

Both turned as Megan dashed out of the front door.

"Megan! How many times have I told you not to let that screen door slam?" Miriam's voice carried outside.

Megan stepped off the porch, leaving a trail of candy pieces. Her soft strawberry curls bounced up and down. "You're home, finally."

Nhaya felt the tugs on her heartstrings. She knelt down and waited for Megan, who had spanned the sidewalk in three steps. Nhaya measured Megan's height by how far the Raggedy Ann doll she always carried hung to the ground. One week away shouldn't have made a difference Nhaya made a big fuss.

"I have grown an inch haven't I. Mom said so. She said you wouldn't even notice."

"Well, that's not so." Nhaya looked up to see her mother watching at the door.

"You remember me?" Adam took a step toward her and Megan promptly slid behind Nhaya.

"What's with the shyness?" Nhaya circled Megan in her arms protectively. "Megan, you know Adam. You just forgot. He has been gone for a while." Nhaya coaxed her out. "It's not like her to shy away from anyone."

Adam smiled. "It's okay. We'll be best friends again."

"My word, girl"—Nhaya turned Megan around— "you have grown again. I was already gone one week!"

Megan grinned her toothy grin. "The yardstick says I'm one inch taller." She yanked at Nhaya's shirt. "Can I have my birthday present now?"

Megan hadn't forgotten. Nhaya reached behind her seat and pulled out the pack.

"I can see you two have important business to do." Adam touched the tip of Megan's little stubbed nose before she could object. Megan wiped her face in disgust. "I'll be back in an hour." He ignored Megan's protest as his large hand covered the top of

Megan's head, ruffling her strawberry curls. "Happy Birthday, squirt! I hope you grow up to be just like your sister."

Nhaya laughed. "What does that mean?" Nhaya walked Adam to his convertible. "I am not a spoiled brat."

"Well, it's a little late, but happy birthday, Megan." Nhaya bent down, scooping her sister up and holding her close. "I missed you! I can't believe you're six years old now!"

"You said you'd get me anudder dolly. Did you?" Megan reached for her backpack.

"No, honey, I went to camp. You don't shop at camp. The word is another. I'm sorry but you will have to wait a little while longer for your present. Where's Mom?"

Megan pouted. "She's busy."

Nhaya took Megan's hand and side-by-side they walked up the front steps.

"We have to wait summore, Gretchen," Megan explained things speaking to her doll. "You will get a little sister soon."

Nhaya pulled the screen door open. The odor of fresh pine and soap greeted her. Miriam peered out from the kitchen at the end of the living room and smiled. Nhaya's guard relaxed. Her mother didn't seem upset. Nhaya removed her shoes before walking across the newly scrubbed wooden floor and began replacing the rugs that were still rolled up.

Her mother stepped out of the sunny yellow kitchen, wiping her hands on the already food-spattered apron. "I was just finishing up a batch of peanut butter cookies for you and Meg."

"I could smell them even outside." Nhaya smiled. She waited in anticipation needing her mother to cross the floor, sweep her into her arms, and give her a warm welcome like Megan had.

All she said was, "We missed you, Nhaya," and then stepped back into the kitchen.

Nhaya's disappointment must have shown, at least to Megan, because Megan put her hand softly back into Nhaya's hand. "Told ya she was busy," Megan said. "Can we have some cookies now?"

Crossing the polished black and white checkered floor to the refrigerator, Nhaya pulled out a bottle of cold milk and then found two plastic glasses from the second shelf. She slipped in beside Megan onto the bench seat at the wooden kitchen table.

"So, how was camp- did you spend time with Renée?" Miriam went back to drying dishes. She set water on the stove to heat.

"Renée? Not really." *Why did she have to bring up Renée so soon?*

Miriam laid the tea towel down and turned to Megan. "Megan, take your cookie and go outside; your sister and I need to talk." She swatted Megan softly on her backside to help her along.

Megan began to pout. Nhaya knew what was coming next. Nhaya and her mother's "private" conversations seemed to happen more and more, and Megan was always shooed out.

"You take care of Gretchen?" Megan handed Nhaya her doll. "And don't drop 'er."

"Megan, the word is her, not 'er. You are not a baby anymore.

"You just turned six," Miriam corrected. She waited for the sound of the screen door to slam before she spoke again. "I got a call from Renée's mother."

"Oh great!" Nhaya felt like Renée must have; a trapped rat in a corner with nowhere to run. She wanted to be first to tell her mother what happened. She sat in silence, again, as she had in the counselor's office.

Miriam looked at Nhaya, waiting for some sort of response. "I suppose the detention you did at camp was punishment enough." She removed her apron and sat across the table from Nhaya. "I know you and Renée have something going on between you, and I don't really care, but I do want you to know the Nez Perce involvement at camp had nothing to do with me not wanting you to go."

So, her mother confirmed it. She had known!

"Then why didn't you tell me? Renée knew all about it, and I looked totally stupid. Mom. It's my culture! I should have known about it, too."

"I should have told you, I am sorry for that, but you- you are so obsessed with this 'birthright' thing. Nhaya, I have told you over and over, we are all just Americans."

"Mom, I know I'm an American but my bloodline is Indian, even if only a fourth. It's me on the inside." Nhaya pointed to her heart. "You used to be proud of our heritage, too, didn't you? What happened?"

Miriam stared at Nhaya before turning her face away. "Your father spent so much time with this passion for his heritage, trying to turn you into him, that he had nothing left for the rest of us."

"Oh, so now this is all my fault?"

Miriam was silent. Nhaya saw the look of weariness come over her face. Composing herself, Miriam drew a cup from the cupboard and poured herself some tea. Nhaya waited, but she already knew what her mother was going to say.

"Nhaya," Miriam's voice softened, "The old world just doesn't exist anymore, and I'm sorry for that. But this is the real world now, right here, not living in the forest with a bow and arrow reliving legends and tales. You need to grow up."

"I still want to be a part of Dad's life.'

"You can. Just keep it real."

Nhaya couldn't be quiet. "Well, mom, the subject is not closed for me!" It will never be over for me. Did you ever love Dad?"

"THAT'S ENOUGH!" Tears suddenly filling her eyes, "you know nothing about how I feel. I loved your father very much. You think life is all about you? Well, it's not. Don't you ever say that to me. Ever!"

"I'm sorry mom. I didn't mean it. I don't know what I want." Nhaya threw up her hands. "I just – what I really need is for the week to start over again. Nhaya turned and fled up the stairs. Tears of frustration ran down her cheeks. Throwing herself down on the bed, Nhaya sobbed. "Things will never be the same! Dad, why did you have to die?"

CHAPTER TEN

*N*haya stared into the bathroom mirror. The emptiness in her soul stared back at her. Looking into the oval-shaped mirror above the pedestal basin. *"I will never, ever, bring up my father's heritage or his name in this house again!"*

Nhaya dabbed a cool washcloth over red, swollen eyes and then splashed her face with cold water.

Returning to her room, she hurriedly put on her newest swimsuit and brushed her hair in quick strokes. Adam would be there any minute. It was too late to change her plans. She had to get down the stairs and outside before Adam came to the door. He didn't need to get involved in her problems.

As she worked her hair into a loose braid, she noticed the new frown lines creasing her brow. What was she thinking, planning another outing without asking? If her mother made a scene, she would never be able to face Adam again.

With one last look in the mirror above her dresser, she adjusted her bathing suit's thin shoulder straps. Her reflection in the mirror surprised her. The new French-cut suit was flattering. Monica had chosen the suit for her earlier that summer. She wouldn't have chosen the pale blue color, and the bottom would have been skirted. But she had toned up from the calisthenics at camp, and her tanned skin made the suit stand out even more striking. Turning sideways, she smiled. Missing a few meals at camp hadn't hurt either. She tucked her necklace away in a place from prying eyes. Looking at the bared space on her neck, she decided to leave the strings on her new peasant blouse loosened, showing off more of her tan.

She was about to leave when an odor drifted into her room. She had smelled it before somewhere. She looked around trying to identify the source of the unusual scent. Nothing seemed different. Perplexed, she opened her closet door, knelt, and sniffed the cotton rugs that covered the hardwood floors. There were no new packages from eccentric Aunt Bessie waiting for her. Perhaps the smell was coming from outside. Nhaya leaned out over the windowsill and looked down. Adam's car was approaching.

The hawk's raspy cry was unforgettable. Its piercing screech echoed through the gables along the roof. Nhaya jumped back, bumping her head on the top of the window. Perched on a branch in the elm tree beside the bedroom window, Nhaya stared at the bird's black beady eyes which seemed to be looking at her. Nhaya gasped!

That's impossible, Nhaya whispered. *How do you know where I live"* She remembered the ring What did she do with it? The bird's stout razor sharp talons were like raptor's claws clutching and unclutching the tree limb as if ready to take flight.

For safety. She used the excuse to hastily grab the shutters and pull them shut. The hawk flew away.

Grabbing her jeans and a beach towel, Nhaya hastened down the stairs. Halfway down, she stopped and groaned. Her mother wasn't about to let her go anywhere, especially after what just happened. *Why does everything in life have to be so darn complicated?*

Nhaya turned and ran back up the stairs and leaned out the window hoping Adam would see her and not come to the door. Waving her hands wildly, she caught his attention. When he looked up, she waved again. *Now, how can I get downstairs without being seen?* "The big Elm." Although she had never attempted the daring feat herself, she watched Megan climb up and down the old tree dozens of times. Turning around, she quietly went to the door, closed it, and picked up her things.

Nhaya opened the window and looked around making sure the hawk was nowhere to be seen. Then with extreme caution, she looked down. *I could do this.* "Mom will never know, and I'll be back before dinner."

Dropping her towel, she watched it fall to the grass below. It was at least twenty feet down. Nhaya's hands turned clammy as she held her breath and gingerly stepped out onto the sturdy branch. This was no time for cowards. She inched her way toward the tree's main trunk and grabbed for it. She felt a little silly standing in the tree. *This was really being "out on a limb".* If she were to get caught, there would be unimaginable consequences. Nevertheless, Nhaya began her decent one branch at a time, skillfully maneuvering her way through the leaf-covered limbs to the ground and to freedom.

Nhaya stayed close to the corner of the house and the side of the porch before she made a beeline to the car. Crouching down like a thief in the night, she slinked across the front yard grass below the window level in case her mother might be in the living room.

Surprised, Adam looked up just as Nhaya threw open the car door and let herself in. He whistled in surprised appreciation.

"Where did you come from? I turned my head away for a moment and you appeared. And you know that's my job."

"What?"

"Opening the door for you."

"Oh. Well, we don't have much time." She laughed, then slumped down in the seat. "Let's go!"

"You have everything?" Adam asked before leaving the curb.

"Yes," she said, shading her eyes and briefly sweeping the sky for signs of the hawk.

"Why are you hiding?" Adam asked. "I'm not. I'm just a little... tired."

"Sure you want to go?"

"Of course."

Adam pulled the car back over to the sidewalk.

"Okay, what's bothering you?" He put his hand on her shoulder. "Everything's not okay; I can see it. What happened to the girl I was with an hour ago?"

"She's still here. Can I ask you a question?"

"Of course. You don't need permission."

"Did you see a large bird fly out from that tree just a few minutes ago while you were waiting for me?" Nhaya pointed to the second story window by her bedroom.

"That's your question? Did I notice a bird? What kind of bird?"

"A hawk!" Nhaya became impatient.

"A hawk?" No, I don't think so, but I wasn't looking at the sky. I had better things to look at—like you. I had forgotten just how beautiful you are. It's hard keeping my eyes off you."

"Adam, I'm serious." She wasn't used to his teasing.

"So was I."

Nhaya crossed her arms.

"Really Serious, huh? No- I haven't seen any hawks, eagles, or dragons today."

"Please don't tease me. Can we please just drive and I'll tell you." Adam drove, half listening.

Nhaya started. "Okay, here's the thing, and I know it sounds ridiculous, so be prepared. I keep seeing this bird everywhere I go. It started at camp a couple of days ago. This bird flew into the window of a cabin." She chose not to mention it was the counselor's cabin. "I thought it was somebody's pet. I mean…you never see a bird fly into a house. If one does, they say it's very bad luck."

"I'll say, birdie crap all over the place." Adam smirked.

"Can you just be quiet until I'm finished! Then it was sitting outside the kitchen door a couple of nights late on top of the camp's trash cans where I was doing KP duty. It kept squawking at me." Nhaya waited. Adam was still silent and trying not to show his humor.

"Okay. So today when we left the bus station, that same bird was sitting on a telephone wire." Nhaya cleared her throat. "I just saw it again next to my bedroom window. Honest. Cross my heart. It was watching me!"

Adam's earnestness turned to humor. "And now, the Twilight Zone... Dooo dooo dooo, dooo," Adam sang the tune to the late night's sci-fi flick. Nhaya was not amused.

"Okay, what makes you think it's the same bird?" Adam questioned.

"Because it has the same distinct markings, and you don't usually see a red-tailed hawk this far north." She hesitated for a moment. "It acts like it knows me. It found my house."

"It knows you." Adam looked over at her.

Nhaya pulled out the gold ring from her pocket. "The bird left this on the table in the counselor's office." Nhaya reached over and handed it to him.

"Counselor's office?" Adam gave her a suspicious look. He took the ring. "It looks like a wedding ring with wings etched inside. Where would a bird get it?"

"How should I know? I didn't ask."

"Touché. Maybe it's following you around because it wants its ring back? Its mate must be miffed!" Adam joked.

Nhaya bristled at the remark but wondered if it was true. The whole conversation was so ridiculous. A bird stalking her for a ring it left on the table. There were many types of birds in the wilds of Idaho. She had learned their names and spent time watching them and their habits. They busied themselves building nests and foraging for food. None of them had given her a second glance. But this bird—she still couldn't deny it. She felt it was following— more like stalking her.

CHAPTER ELEVEN

*A*dam drove the country road in silence. The Pack River Lumber Mill came into view. "My father used to work there, along with most of the other 400 men who lived here in Dover," Nhaya said.

Adam nodded when she pointed to the broken-down mill. He let her tell the story again, although he remembered the incident very well. Her father's arm had been crushed when the chain holding two thousand pounds of logs broke, spilling them into the river. Her father was pinned between the chain and a log. Several other men were trapped under water. Nine men died that day, including Nhaya's father. The lumber mill was shut down due to faulty equipment and strict codes that had not been followed.

"Since the mill closed in Dover," Nhaya explained, "people started leaving to find jobs elsewhere. Most of the houses in our neighborhood are vacant now. Not one new shop has opened since you've been gone, Adam. I find that quite pathetic. How about the rest of us who are stuck here? Now we have to go into Sandpoint just to do any real shopping."

Adam sighed. "Actually, that's what I like best about Dover. It's so quiet."

"It's great for old people," Nhaya said.

"Hey, I plan on living here for the rest of my life." Adam chuckled.

"I hope you'll be happy." Nhaya's voice dripped with sarcasm. Adam rolled with laughter.

"I can't even imagine you wanting to waste your life here."

He patted her shoulder. "I don't really mean right here but somewhere in Northern Idaho. I've been to Europe and places back east. Everything I could possibly want is right here." Adam glanced at her then gave her arm a gentle squeeze.

The comment went right over Nhaya's head. She was picturing places she would like to live, and Dover wasn't one of them. Adam turned up the radio and began to sing along—off key. Nhaya stared out her window trying not to giggle.

It had been miserable living in the outer fringes of town until she discovered Sandpoint seven miles west of Dover. It was everything she had heard about it; a beautiful resort town on the end of the most beautiful lake she had ever seen. The locals played volleyball every weekend on the white sand that encircled part of the bay. But for her, seven miles might as well have been seventy when there was no transportation to get there. Sandpoint was where she had met Monica. The two had become instant friends.

Adam turned the steering wheel sharply, causing the car to swerve, breaking her thoughts, and bringing her back to the present. "My singing bothering you?" he teased. "We're almost there."

The car swung onto the narrow one-way street that dead-ended at the lodge on the lakefront. The street was crowded with tourists wearing every type of clothing from classic sundresses to swimwear. The quaint little shops displayed racks of marked down, red-tagged merchandise outside. Adam slowed the car to a crawl as tourists wandered off and onto the sidewalks, jaywalking to catch the next sale. Nhaya liked looking at the sale tables herself, oblivious to the many envious stares at Adam and his vintage car. She looked for Monica among the crowd. The sales would still be there tomorrow. She would find a great gift for Megan.

Although she had seen it many times before, the beautiful sight, which lay ahead, took Nhaya's breath away. The MG rolled to a stop right in front of the lake view Nhaya had loved all her life. The mid- afternoon water in the cove laid serene, glass- like and mirroring back the white sails from the small boats anchored there. It felt like home.

"If you're thinking how beautiful this is," Adam remarked, "I feel the same way. I never get tired of being here. We used to have a lot of fun chasing each other around on this beach."

Nhaya opened the car door without taking her eyes off the view and unlaced her shoes, smiling contently. "Thanks for bringing me, Adam. This is just what I needed." The white sand stirred beneath her feet as she sprinted toward the volleyball game in session, Adam following at her heels.

"Hey," Nhaya waved to someone she recognized. "Do you have room for two more. If so, which side do you want us on?"

Nhaya felt the strength leave her legs. She stumbled in the sand, losing the point to the other team. She rubbed at her injured wrist handing the ball to Adam.

"You okay?"

"Yeah. Too much fun at camp, I guess. I'm going to go get a drink."

Nhaya dropped down in front of the cooler, grateful that Adam had remembered to bring one. She plunged her aching wrist deep into the icy water and pulled out a frosty bottle of Coke and popped off the top. The ice soothed her sore wrist and the welcomed fizz burned her throat as she gulped it down. With her thirst satisfied, she laid back and stared at the white and blue tapestry.

Sandpoint's famous lake surrounded by miles of evergreens also had a cove with a crescent-shaped sandy beach. After an hour of volleyball and her wrist soaking in water cold as a mountain stream, she laid back and surveyed the blue sky being covered with large fluffy white clouds hiding the sun. She closed her eyes.

Nhaya opened one eye and squinted upward. The sound of seagulls squawking their talk became annoying. *Those pesky white birds* She watched a group of them dip and rise with the air currents. It seemed strange to her to see ocean-dwelling birds in Idaho. She scanned the sky again for her hawk until she was satisfied it wasn't around. Her Aunt Bessie was very adamant about bids.

Birds are omens; they bring warning signs to the those who listen. Her father had also told her to always pay close attention to nature. *Nature can tell us things.* Perhaps the irritating gulls were miffed about something too; probably asking why they were circling this lake instead of soaring high over an ocean beach catching crabs.

She watched Adam batting the ball across the net. He seemed to be having the time of his life, no cares, covered from head to toe with sand. His arms and legs were browned by the sun, but the rest of his body was pale, a classic farmer's tan. Feelings for him stirred inside her. It was more than being excited that Adam was home. Maybe she was just lonely. Seeing Justin in the flesh, revived the sting of rejection. She could pretend all she wanted, but Justin had never paid attention to her after the first day.

Adam was changing, even more so. It was the way he looked at her, and earlier, he alluded to hanging out as a date. They were still good buddies, but now he was making her feel self-conscious. When he picked her up out of the car, she knew she blushed. It would be way too awkward to be more than friends.

She imagined kissing Adam. After shaking her head in rejection, she drained another bottle of pop. When She looked up,

Adam was staring at her again. He winked at her! Nhaya blushed. Was she talking to herself again?

Things used to be different. The games that kids played like hide and seek were for fun. Now it wasn't just a game – and there were no rules on how you play the games– just eliminate your opponent if necessary. Not 'kiss' them. She still believed that Justin liked her. Whatever Brenda said, it was her thoughts not his.

"Nhaya you are back!"

Nhaya looked up. Monica was calling out to her from the parking lot. She sprinted barefoot easily through the soft sand toward her.

The scene put an image in Nhaya's mind of Monica in a TV commercial. Her tall perfect form, dark tanned skin -- add long honey blond hair that bounced in step to her glide. As she grew closer, the new red two-piece swimsuit they had shopped together for, completed the show. Heads turned! Including Adam's! Nhaya felt a tinge of jealously. Game on?

As soon as Monica reached Nhaya, she dropped her bag and a white floppy hat on Nhaya's laid out towel. Nhaya reached up and gave her a hug.

"Hey, look at you! Love the swimsuit on you we found. I was right about the color. It was about time you got a new one. That one piece suit you have been wearing was so outdated. It's the 80's now. Styles have changed.

"Is there ever a place you go where you don't make heads turn?" Nhaya asked. Monica's laughter was melodic.

"Told you Nhy, it's the new fashions. Besides, you don't even see the guys gawking at you. I'd kill for your hair. Few keep their natural hair color these days And I can count on one hand the girls that have silky black natural hair. You are beautiful girl. Look in the mirror occasionally."

Nhaya dusted loose sand from her legs. She felt Monica was just being sweet. After all, being five foot six was average. Everything about her was average.

Nhaya twisted her fingers lightly through her hair, a quirky habit she often did when she was nervous or when she was embarrassed. Sometimes when she was lost in thought. She studied Monica's face. Her Coppertone tan did look a bit orange. She was lucky to have her father's easily tanned skin.

Her best feature, she thought to herself, were her eyes—maybe because her grandmother told her that when she was little. the gray blue of her eyes were the color of the Artic Grey wolf. Her Aunt Bessie was an artist and painted the beautiful wolves after studying them in the wild.

She couldn't compare herself with the girls at the beach. Most of them were bleached blondes, taking advantage of the latest hair styles. She looked at her slim hands and natural nails. If one of her friends were to break a polished nail on the ball they were spiking, it would be considered a catastrophe!

She had always been considered a tomboy and, actually, she preferred to hang out with mostly guys. Adam said he liked a little meat on his girl's bones. She wasn't heavy by any means, but she wasn't a size two either.

"Nhaya!" Monica said, turning over, "where'd you go, girl?" She broke into Nhaya's revere. "You know, I'm really sorry I wasn't at camp this week. It was my dad's week, and he wanted us to do something together." Monica reached into her bag for a bottle of baby oil. "Funny, Dad has never cared about spending time with me before," Monica said without thought.

After Monica was adequately oiled and her head dawned with the floppy hat, which covered most of her face, she settled in for some gossip. "So, tell me about camp."

"It was…"—Nhaya searched for the right words— "one I wouldn't want to relive."

"Ooh, that bad? Really missed me, huh?" Monica giggled.

"You have no idea,"

"So- spill."

"Bet you can guess if you think hard." Both chimed in unison, "Renée!" Nhaya laughed like she hadn't laughed in a week.

"Renée has always been a pain in the butt for you. Nhaya."

"We just don't see eye to eye, and this year I really lost my cool."

Monica lay back on her towel after rechecking her arms and chest. "Why you even talk to Renée is a mystery to me."

"I have to be civil to her because of my mother. She and Renée's mother are friends. Besides, she was in my cabin." Nhaya changed the subject. "So…how was it with your dad?"

"My parents have finally decided to get a divorce."

Monica's comment came across as if she didn't care, but Nhaya knew she was devastated.

"The only thing good about it is that with them dividing up the households, I'll probably get some new stuff." Monica laughed non-convincingly as she tossed her hat and began applying oil to her face. "I've always hated hats. Maybe they will be out of style next year." Monica offered the oil to Nhaya.

"Yeah, and maybe, we will be wearing Pedal Pushers again. My mother kept all my clothes. I could be right in style."

"Actually, that's pretty funny." Monic said. "Styles seem to make their way back. I heard there were more people from Hayden at camp. Did Mr. Cool show up?"

"He was with a new girl; a girl I've never seen before."

"I'm sorry." Monica reached out and touched Nhaya's hand.

"It's okay. I'm over him."

"Really? Well, I'm glad if that's true. He is not for you."

"So, I've been told."

"Where's Megan today? Didn't you just get home?" Monica stretched out and adjusted her suit straps for more exposure to the sun.

"She's at home. I came with Adam in his new convertible." She flashed Monica a mischievous little smile.

"He's back?" Monica sat up and scanned the players.

"Adam just started a summer job at the bus terminal. He gave me a ride home from the station, and I asked him if he wanted to hang out here for a while."

Monica tipped her sunglasses, spying Adam over the top of the frames. "He looks different. I almost didn't recognize him." They both watched as Adam spiked the ball.

"I almost didn't recognize him myself at the station. He has filled out."

"He sure isn't a toothpick anymore, Check out his b —!"

"Shhhh. He could hear you." Monica gave a low whistle, and Nhaya jabbed her in the ribs. "He referred to this afternoon as us on a date. I'm not sure how I feel about being more than friends. That's what we have always been. It's just nice to have him back."

"You could sure do a lot worse." Monica watched him.

"Adam told Brenda he had a crush on me. Do you think that's true?"

"Well, it's easier for someone who isn't so close to see it." Nhaya studied Adam more as he played. He acted differently. He had self-confidence. He didn't brag about his car. Instead, he just drove it. Adam's charm wasn't in what he said, it was in what he didn't say. Nhaya felt she could trust him with anything. She knew Adam was loyal. He had come to her defense many times.

Nhaya sat back and began to laugh. She had just composed a mental list for her hero: a great bod, charming, loyal, and into her. Maybe she had been looking in the wrong places after all.

Nhaya remembered the magazine article from the bus ride home in *"True Love Magazine. "Be Best Friends First."* Nhaya questioned her feelings again.

"What are you laughing about?" Monica asked.

Nhaya waved her off. "Honestly, just life in general. Oh, by the way, I have something for you. I found some varieties of mushrooms for your botany class. You can dry them for next year."

"You picked them at camp?"

Suddenly Nhaya perked up. "You really missed out on camp this time. A group of Nez Perce men joined us. The theme for camp this year was 'Living One with Nature.' We took a hike with a man named Joe Eagle Feather and learned about plants and herbs that were used in their tribes. The flowers used for dyes, and certain herbs used years ago for medicinal purposes that no longer exist. Some things were even new to me, and that's when I found the most interesting species of mushrooms."

"Did you bring them with you?"

"No, I didn't even know you'd be here today. I looked for you when we drove through town, thought you'd be bargain hunting. There are a lot of end-of-summer sales going on. Let's hang out tomorrow. We can meet at the Ice Cream Shoppe. I still have so much to tell you!"

Monica nodded her approval. "Sounds like a plan. My mom gave me twenty bucks yesterday. That will buy me several shirts if everything's on sale. Don't you still need to buy something for Meg? If I remember, her birthday was yesterday…"

The breeze changed abruptly into gusts of wind. Monica's hat went flying. Nhaya reached out and grabbed it as it flew by her. Something told her she needed to get home and it wasn't the sudden weather change. Looking up at the billowing black clouds approaching rapidly from the far side of the lake meant a summer lightning storm could rise fast. Idaho droughts brought frightening forest fires caused by lightning.

Monica was still chattering.

Nhaya swallowed, beginning to feel sick. There was a bad feeling beginning in the pit of her stomach. It resembled the feeling she had when she was caught doing something wrong. Had her mother figured out she was gone?

"Speaking of mushrooms…" Monica had never stopped talking. "I wished I could've been at camp. I've learned some pretty cool things myself in botany this summer. Did you know all most 100% of the mushrooms in the wild are poisonous? We studied some actual cases where people have eaten them by mistake."

"I'm sorry…what did you say?" Nhaya picked up on the word poison.

"In one case, thirty-one children died from eating mushrooms served in their school cafeteria!" Monica recited the statistics. "And a Korean woman living in Oregon picked some mushrooms that looked like the ones she picked as a child in Korea. Out of the five people she fed them to, four had to have liver transplants. Even mushrooms like morels can make you super sick if they are the wrong variety. A couple of days after the poison mushrooms are consumed, the person is- toast." Monica snapped her fingers.

"Seriously? I didn't know that. Mushrooms. Even in Idaho?"

"Yeah. Most are in the wilderness. Keep them put away until. tomorrow. We can examine them then. Did Joe Eagle Feather show you which ones were okay to pick?"

"Well, actually, they didn't want us to pick anything, but I thought it was more for the environment, not that they might be harmful. I doubt anyone in my family would be interested in them; we all hate mushrooms."

Adam had walked up on them unnoticed. He grabbed a soda from the cooler and squatted down between them. "What are you two talking about?"

Monica turned to him. "Adam, hey, it's great to see you again. I hardly recognized you over there. Are you back for good?" Monica inquired.

"Yep. I missed this old town." He touched Nhaya's leg as he spoke.

Monica caught his meaning, but Nhaya's thoughts where still on Monica's fears.

"So, what's the score?" Monica lifted her sunglasses.

"Four to one—us!" Adam chugged the entire contents of his bottle and let out a large belch.

"Gross!" Monica distanced herself from him. "Nhaya, is this Adam's new charm?"

Nhaya's smile was forced. "He's always been this way." Her thoughts were calculating Monica's statistics: At a school, thirty-one children had died from eating mushrooms. Out of a family of five children, four children had to have liver transplants.

The volleyball suddenly landed in front of Monica, flinging sand on her.

"Hey, can one of you get back over here? Our team is uneven," Jon called from the grass court.

Adam wrapped his hand around Nhaya's arm pulling her up. "We're coming! C'mon Nhaya, let's save their day."

"I actually should get home, Adam. Megan will want her birthday present, and I don't have one yet."

"You are tired of my company already?"

"Don't be silly. I just need to see Megan and spend some time with her. too."

Adam checked the time. "I've got to work the late shift anyway. But you still owe me another hour."

"Okay, sure." Nhaya jumped up, pulling on her jeans. "I just need to make a quick call. Can we stop by the hotel and use the payphone first?"

"Sure, but we're only twenty minutes away from your house, in this car, he winked- even sooner."

"I know, but I just need to talk to my mom for a sec to make sure everything's okay." If she called now maybe she could lessen her punishment instead of coming home unaware that she had been caught. After Monica's study on mushrooms and knowing her sister's appetite for adventure, she wondered if Megan would rummage through her stuff and find them.

"What could possibly go wrong in an hour?" Adam asked.

Probably nothing - almost anything - after the week I just had," she laughed. "Just feel I need to give her a quick call. I left so abruptly, I didn't even get a chance to talk to her or Megan."

The wind gusted and blew trash out of a nearby can, tumbling it across the parking lot. Nhaya quickly picked up her towel observing the blackening sky. "Monica," Nhaya called out, "I've gotta go." Nhaya hugged her arms as thunder grumbled in the distance. "I can't remember closing the door to my room. I am worried about Megan getting into my camping stuff. She is such a sneak."

Monica slipped on her flip flops and wrapped herself up in her towel. "I didn't mean to make you paranoid." She apologized as she ran beside Nhaya.

Adam reached the car first, pushing the release button inside the car to raise the top. "It looks like we're in for that thunderstorm sooner than they predicted."

All three looked around. Someone was already untying the strings on the volleyball net and everyone was heading to their cars. "You know, Megan," Nhaya said as they walked a little faster toward their car. "She is always getting into my stuff. I left to come here in such a hurry, I didn't put anything away. If Adam hadn't just got home, I would have stayed with her today. She'll be looking for her birthday present. I promised to bring her something."

"I hardly think Megan would be interested in a bunch of shriveled up mushrooms."

"You're probably right, but I still need to get home. My mom and I had a fight earlier," Nhaya confessed. "And then I left without her knowing."

"Oops." Monica murmured.

Adam opened the passenger door for Nhaya and stood waiting.

"Call me when you can," Monica called out, backing away.

CHAPTER TWELVE

*A*chily gust of air blew through the open window in Nhaya's upstairs bedroom. Miriam stood beside it; her thin shaped lips pressed tight together. Absentmindedly, her fingers pushed back the few stray hairs that escaped from her thick loosely woven hair that cascaded off her shoulder. Miriam shook her head.

"What was in your mind Nhaya. Why would you do such a stupid thing climbing down this tree" How could she ever make her daughter understand that she wasn't the enemy?

Miriam walked back to Megan's room. She pulled out another blanket from the closet and draped it across her. Miriam frowned. Though asleep, the child tossed and turned, her legs in restless motion. Touching Megan's forehead, she thought Megan had a slight fever. Megan had already contracted had chickenpox so it was doubtful she had it again. It was also unlikely she had been exposed to mumps or even a virus. Whatever it was, she had come down with it quickly.

From the window, Miriam watched as the delicate petals from her favorite rosebush skittered across the lawn. She also checked the road in hopes that Nhaya was with Adam. She would be safe with him. If she wasn't so worried about Megan, she would be out driving the streets herself.

The unusual color of the sky told Miriam they could be in for a whopper of a lightning storm. Thousands of acres of forest lands were destroyed every year, along with wildlife due to dry lightning storms. Miriam wrapped her sweater closer around her shoulders, feeling the chill.

The storm was building with force. Feeling the weight of her day, Miriam decided to call her sister. She needed a change; they all needed a change. Spending a few weeks in Montana might do all three of them some good. It had been hard raising two kids alone and losing her husband had been hardest on Nhaya.

Before heading downstairs to call Bessie, Miriam decided to brew herself a cup of tea. Besides needing a break, her nerves felt on edge, ready to shatter! She made her way over to the sink and began filling the teapot with cold water, her mind somewhere between Nhaya and Megan.

Glancing through the kitchen window, she noticed a large stocky bird sitting on the support pole of her clothesline. The bird spread its large wings against the wind. Miriam could see its stubby red-tail feathers. *"A hawk, a red-tailed hawk?"*

Over the years, her family had collected many red-tailed hawk feathers. Prized for their rare beauty, they were used in the ceremonial war bonnet and carried great cultural significance.

Miriam moved closer to the window hoping to get a better look at the magnificent creature. The hawk flexed and tightened its claws, anchoring itself on the pole. Miriam stared at the bird as it settled in. *What was it doing here?* The bird seemed to want to stay. She kept an eye it is wondering if it might be wounded.

Nhaya pressed the payphone against her ear to drown out the noise in the lobby of the hotel restaurant. The phone rang several times at the house before her mother answered. She took a deep breath. "Mom, it's me."

"Where on earth are you?" Miriam's voice sounded more worried than angry.

"I'm at the Lake Shore Hotel, Mom. Adam drove me. I'm really sorry. I had already told him I could go to the beach. I thought you wouldn't let me go, and I didn't want him to see us fighting."

"We'll talk later. There's a bad storm coming this way. Come home now."

"I know. I'll be there in a few minutes. Has Megan been in my room?"

"No. Megan is sick."

"Sick! How?"

"Nhaya, I don't know. She took a nap and then woke up a little while ago with a terrible headache. When I went into her room, her covers were drenched with sweat. I can't remember either of you kids ever running such a high fever. I was about call the doctor when you called."

"Mom, are you sure she didn't get into my room?"

"I don't have any idea." Miriam had become inpatient

"I just didn't want her to get into my stuff from camp."

"Nhaya, that's the least of my worries. Just get yourself home. Now!"

"Okay. Okay, I'm coming."

A bolt of lightning struck again, hitting somewhere close to the shore making a deafening, crackling noise. Nhaya held tight to the wood railing on the restaurant stairs as she hurried down to Adam, who was waiting patiently for her at the door.

"Boy that was a close one. How's everything at home?"

"It's not good." Nhaya began crying. "Megan has gotten sick suddenly. Mom's calling the doctor. I should never have left."

"Well, it certainly can't be your fault," Adam said.

"Please just drive."

Neither spoke as Adam sped through town. Nhaya watched the wind's growing forces rip off the tender leaves from newly planted trees. Shoppers were rushing to their cars and storekeepers were busy pulling clothes off tables and racks.

The ride home lasted only about half the time it took to get to the beach. Nhaya didn't say a word about Adam's driving, and Adam hadn't apologized as he ran several stop signs. The look on Nhaya's face had been all it took to make him rush.

Overhead, the long fingers of lightening flashed across the darkening sky. Each time it cracked, the thunder came closer and sounding like an explosion. Adam pulled up in front of the house and turned on his wipers, erasing the first few drops of rain from the windshield that had begun.

Nhaya noticed a strange car parked in front of her home. "This storm will be a good test to see if this rag top is waterproof." Adam reached over from his seat for her door, but Nhaya had beaten him to it.

"Can you get in okay?" Adam asked.

"I'll be fine, thanks."

"Please be sure to let me know about Megan."

Nhaya hugged Adam.

"You think birds are chasing you, and you are acting very strange. I can't get anything out of you worth listening to, so I will wait till you can call me with some answers if you actually have any. The car sped away.

Throwing the towel over her head, she stepped away from the car, dodging the growing puddles. "I'll call you as soon as I know anything!" Nhaya hollered and ran across the lawn.

Adam was right. Maybe too much time had passed. He had never questioned her before. *Adam, why can't you just be the guy used I know?*

The bang of the front screen door brought Miriam out of the upstairs bedroom. Nhaya looked toward the top landing. Her mother stood there waiting, wringing her hands as she shifted her weight from foot to foot. Her eyes told Nhaya everything she didn't want to know.

"Doctor Telford is here."

He thinks it could be Megan's appendix." Miriam told her.

Nhaya raced up the stairs to Megan's room. It was vacant. "Mom"— Nhaya's eyes were wild with fear— "I'm sorry I left without telling you. Where is Megan?"

"She's in my room." Miriam pointed and moved out of the way to let Nhaya pass. "The doctor is with her."

Miriam picked up the soiled blanket from the floor. "I had to clean Megan's bed. She threw up several times."

Nhaya took a deep breath before she entered. "Hey, sweetie," Nhaya whispered, trying to hide the panic that gripped her. She touched Megan's forehead.

"The ambulance is here," Doctor Telford said. He slipped his stethoscope back into the black leather bag. "I'll make the call to the hospital and arrange for a room. Good to see you, Nhaya." He patted her arm.

Nhaya took his place and sat down on the bed. Megan whimpered when she saw Nhaya.

"I'm here now, honey." Nhaya bent over and tried to cradle her.

The door opened again and both Miriam and the doctor came back in. Megan drew herself closer to Nhaya."

"No!" Megan pouted.

"He's here to help you." Nhaya guided Megan's head back against the pillow.

"No!" Megan squealed and tried to sit up.

Nhaya and Megan watched as Doctor Telford reached inside his bag and produced a bottle of medicine and a syringe exposing a large silver needle. Nhaya swallowed hard as Doctor Telford inserted the needle into the medicine bottle.

A moment later, Megan tried to free herself from her sister's grip. Nhaya cringed and held Megan as the needle penetrated Megan's hip. Her mother stepped in to help hold Megan down. The scream could be heard outside.

Nhaya cradled Megan, holding her tightly. "It's okay now," she whispered. She knew Megan was more frightened than hurt.

"I'm going to ride to the hospital with Megan," Nhaya's mother informed her. "You stay close to the phone, and I'll call you as soon as I know anything,"

"Mom, I need to come, too," Nhaya protested.

"Do as I ask, Nhaya, please. I'll call you when I find out anything."

"I have to come," Nhaya insisted. "I wasn't there when Dad…"

"Honey"—her mother soothed her. This isn't the same thing that happened to your father. Megan will be okay, I promise."

Doctor Telford checked Megan's pulse. Nhaya looked up at him with questioning eyes. "She is going to be okay.," Doctor Telford said with an assuring smile.

The screen door slammed again. This time the paramedics brought up the stretcher.

"We need to step away so the medics can do their job." The doctor escorted Nhaya and her mother down the stairs.

Megan whimpered. Then there was silence. Nhaya squeezed her mother's hand as the paramedics carried the stretcher downstairs with Megan lying limp beneath its covers.

The doctor patted Miriam on the shoulder. "I gave Megan a little sedative. I figured both of you needed it. It just took a few minutes to work. She's in good hands."

Outside, Nhaya clutched at her jacket and walked closely beside Megan. Miriam's skirt whipped in the wind. One of the paramedics helped Miriam up into the back of the ambulance. Then the door slammed behind her, and with the shriek of the siren, Megan and her mother sped away. Nhaya stood alone, pelted by the rain.

Nhaya's legs were heavy with the weight of worry as she dragged herself back up the stairs to her room. Her bedroom door was closed tight. She turned the knob and peered in. Nothing seemed out of place. She kicked off her tennis shoes and propped them up on the floor heater to dry. After peeling off her rain-soaked shirt, she sat down on the floor next to her backpack. It sat in its upright position against her bedpost just where she had left it, untouched.

Very thankful, Nhaya curled up with a blanket and shivered. Tears began to run down her face. She needed to be with her family. Her "old companion" guilt pointed out that it was she who left them, not the other way around. Nhaya began to sob. Things just weren't fair.

CHAPTER THIRTEEN

*N*haya sat up with a start, realizing she had dozed off. Still damp and chilled from standing in the rain, she grabbed fresh socks from the second drawer and padded down the stairs.

The lights in the house flickered off and on from the storm. As she walked about the rooms, the wind howled and whistled outside. Hugging herself, Nhaya shivered. She passed through the kitchen to the laundry room, grabbing a piece of bread on the way. She was famished. Stuffing her mouth, she reached into the dryer, rummaging through the clean clothes and grabbed a shirt and a pair of her jeans.

The rain streamed down the pane of the laundry room window like a vehicle moving through a carwash. Nhaya tried to be positive and not make a monster out of her fear. Time seemed to slow to a snail's pace. Outside, the thunder rolled, but inside the house had a silent emptiness. Funny, she had never noticed the slow methodical tick of the grandfather clock in the hall, nor had she ever listened to the steady beating of her own heart.

The phone rang. Nhaya jumped.

"Mom?" Nhaya said nervously into the phone. She held her breath, waiting and hoping it was her.

"Well, Megan hasn't changed much," her mother said in an unusually calm voice. "They're still doing tests."

"So, it's not her appendix like they thought?" Nhaya said, with hope in her voice.

"No." Miriam sighed. "I wish it was. That's a common problem they are used to dealing with. All the blood work points negative. Now they think it might be something she ate."

"Something she ate?" Nhaya swallowed, her face paled. "Nhaya, I can't, for the life of me, come up with anything that could be poisonous in our house except for the few cleaners under the kitchen sink, and Megan has known forever not to touch those." A cold sweat broke and ran down the crease of Nhaya's back.

Her face went slack. "I can," her words spilled out. "I gotta go, Mom." Nhaya quickly hung up the phone.

Grabbing the handrail, Nhaya bolted up the stairs, two at a time. She felt her foot turn under her and winced. When she forced herself to stand, the pain worsened. She hopped one-footed into her room.

Sitting on the floor, Nhaya dumped the contents of her backpack out onto the braided rug. The pile was full of dirty jeans and socks. The box, created to hold her specimens, was still there. Nhaya held it up and turned it over in her hands. It looked untouched and appeared unlikely Megan had found it. Gently rubbing her ankle, she drew in a huge sigh of relief. She opened the top of the box. How many mushrooms had she picked? Nhaya fingered the different shapes. Not being able to remember, she returned the box to her backpack, hiding it high in her closet.

She rarely went into Megan's room, but she pushed open the door and looked inside. What a war zone! Megan's bed linens were turned upside down, pillows and blankets pushed to the floor. The room smelled of sweat and vomit.

Nhaya tripped on the edge of the new braided rug beside Megan's bed and bent down to straighten it. Something rolled off the rug and fell against her hand. It was grey and wrinkled. She picked it up and held it. It was a partly eaten mushroom.

No, Megan, you didn't! Megan had gotten into her backpack after all. Panic stabbed her heart as she recalled Monica's fatal words at the beach: *Anyone who eats one is already dead!*

"Monica! You can't know everything there is about mushrooms. Not everyone who eats them has to die!"

Nhaya hobbled to her window and dumped out the remaining mushrooms from the box. They disappeared in the darkness of the storm.

"How could this have happened?" Nhaya whispered.

A flash of lightening lit the sky again. Nhaya had the feeling she was being watched again. Brushing her wet hair from her face, she looked across the yard and saw it: the hawk!

"You again!" *What do you want, you stupid bird?*

The hawk took flight but did not fly away. Instead, spreading its great wings, it flew towards her open window!

Nhaya screamed in terror. She turned and fled down the stairs to the living room. Reaching the bottom landing, she dove to the floor, sure that the hawk had pursued her. Scooting backwards into the corner of the room, she wedged herself behind the armchair, hoping she wouldn't be seen.

The hawk looked much larger in flight. Its wings had spanned the entire width of her bedroom window, and its claws that stretched before it, looked like they could grab and tear an animal to shreds!

Birds don't fly into people's houses and attack them. Get a grip Nhaya. Her aunt did once warn her, *"If a bird flies into your house, it means someone in your family will die."* It was the reason her aunt never left a window open without a screen. *It was just a silly superstition- right?*

When the waiting became more than she could bear, Nhaya reached up and grabbed the phone on the table, her fingers trembled as she dialed the hospital number. When someone answered, she whispered, her voice dry and raspy. "You have a patient there, the last name of Winters—Megan Winters. She's six-years-old. The ambulance just brought her in a little while ago. Can you help me find her?"

"Did you call the emergency room?" the attendant asked in a professional tone.

"I don't know that number. Can't you just find it for me?"

"I'll check with emergency. Please hold."

Nhaya waited. The grandfather clock ticked out the minutes. Finally, she hung up, convinced they had forgotten her.

Nhaya bit her lip. Did she dare go back upstairs? The rain was surely pouring through the opened window. She had to close it, and she had to get to the hospital.

Nhaya peeked through the crack behind her open bedroom door: the room was empty, no sight of the demon hawk. Cautiously, she stepped inside quickly shutting the window and then began to calculate her route to the hospital. For her, a few extra miles by way of the back roads would be safer than driving through town. Less traffic.

Gathering up her nerves, shoes, and jacket, Nhaya hurried downstairs and out the kitchen door. Her mother's keys hung on the hook by the backdoor. Before stepping outside, she thought about the consequences of getting caught. There was no turning back once she left. It was bad enough she had climbed out the window but taking her mother's only transportation without permission could be disastrous for her and the car.

Ducking her head, Nhaya sprinted toward the garage. Could she remember everything she had learned about driving from last year? Aunt Bessie had let her use her car to practice but driving up and down her long dirt driveway hadn't prepared her to drive on the road with other cars, lights, pedestrians, and animals running amuck.

She raised the rickety garage door, bringing in gusts of rain. Her mother's old black DeSoto seemed to be waiting obediently for its owner to return.

The car door was unlocked. Nhaya slid in. Her mother only washed the outside occasionally, but the inside of the car was as clean as when the DeSoto was new. Nhaya ran her hands around the steering wheel like her mother always did before starting it. Why did her mother do that? Maybe she was praying for a safe trip, or maybe she was just plain thankful for a reliable vehicle. She turned the key. The car's motor came to life with a low-pitched purr.

Nhaya shoved it into reverse and let the clutch out. Bam! The car lurched backwards, hitting the garbage cans behind her. "Why would you put the trash right smack behind the car? *Mother!*"

Nhaya hit her fists against the steering wheel and turned off the key. "I'll never get used to this stupid clutch!"

Stepping out, Nhaya looked at the back of the car and cringed when she saw a small but obvious scratch on the fender. She cursed. Raising her shirt, Nhaya spit on it and rubbed the scrape in circles. The scratch remained. But of course.

After tossing the empty trash cans aside, she returned to the car, eased in the clutch, shifted into reverse, and let out the clutch— slowly this time. The car rolled backward, clearing the garage. The rain streamed down the windows. Remembering to hold the clutch in, she found the neutral position. With the brake firmly set, she dashed out again, quickly pulling the rickety garage door down.

The lights! She needed lights. Nhaya found the knob and pulled. Two circles of light reflected across the garage door. Exasperated after pulling out two more knobs, which turned out to be the heater and the radio, she discovered the wipers. They began to thump at a quick tempo across the windshield. She rolled down the window and adjusted the side mirror, her twisted ankle aching from holding down the clutch.

Glancing into the rearview mirror, the driveway seemed longer than she remembered. After backing out onto the road, Nhaya congratulated herself and shifted back into first gear. The car lurched forward several times before she shifted into second.

Pulling forward, Nhaya exhaled. Going straight had been easy. Now she had the first turn coming up. Peering through the rain, she watched as the corner grew nearer. She began the turn and was just about to congratulate herself when a back tire scrubbed the curb. She wasn't even out of the neighborhood. Funny, she remembered the bus driver doing the same thing when they pulled into camp. She had thought him a moron, and he was maneuvering a huge bus, not a car.

The DeSoto picked up speed. Nhaya squinted through the streaks of the windshield wipers which fought hard to keep up with the pounding rain, and they were losing.

CHAPTER FOURTEEN

$\mathcal{B}$onner General Hospital was on the outskirts of town. Nhaya watched for car headlights coming from behind and decided she would pull over if anyone got too close to her.

She was grateful when she saw part of the new emergency sign on the top of the Bonner General Hospital. It stood out even in the down poor. Nhaya noticed something else. She had been wrong. Something new had been built. The brick hospital now had two stories. It seemed the number of sick and injured were on the rise.

Nhaya pulled in behind the hospital to the emergency entrance. The back still looked the same. The parking lot behind was almost full. Nhaya checked out the parking spaces. Even though her mother didn't have a handicapped permit, those spaces looked bigger and were closer to the door. She eased the car into the reserved spot and complemented herself on her parking. She felt worthy of a handicapped space. Besides, she wouldn't be long, unless her mother asked too many questions. In that event, she wouldn't have to worry about a parking ticket. She'd be confined to her room until she turned eighteen.

Nhaya remembered to remove the keys and lock the DeSoto's doors. Hopping over puddles, she headed for the faded green and white striped canopy that hung over the entrance to the emergency door. To the left of the door was an ashtray full of half-smoked cigarettes. A sign above read: "NO SMOKING BEYOND THESE DOORS."

Nhaya paused beneath the covering. It was as if time had turned back the clock. She was twelve again, holding onto her mother's hand. She could even remember what she did that day. They were just driving back from her swimming lessons and her mother still had on her kitchen apron. Megan blissfully slept in the backseat of the car.

Nhaya stepped through the emergency doors, fighting off memories of yesterday. A few non-patients were seated, heads bent, waiting. Others paced back and forth down the one narrow hallway between rooms.

The image of her father hanging between the two men, his blood on the white tile floor, still caused her nightmares. She reached out her hand as if to physically touch him and tried to remember the feel of his hard-working, rough hand.

Her father's death had come sudden and unwelcomed. She wasn't able to see him one last time—to say she loved him. Now she was in this same impersonal, disinfected smelling place. She could hardly bear the thought of Megan lying somewhere in a room like her father had. Another thought surfaced. She tried to push it away. Could her mother have saved her father if she had been at home by the phone instead of driving her to a swimming lesson? Although she was told countless times it had nothing to do with her, she still wasn't sure.

Nhaya wrapped her arms around her stomach and moved steadily down the hallway. In her mind, she knew it wasn't the same situation, but the terror wouldn't leave her. What had possessed her to come through the emergency entrance anyway? It was too late now to turn around. She closed her eyes to shield her mind from the vivid scene that would forever haunt her. Her stomach churned several times from the medicinal smells which did little to cover the odor of blood and sickness.

Nhaya kept her head bowed to avoid the inquisitive looks until she could turn the corner to the next hallway.

She rode the elevator to the second floor where the patient's rooms were. If anyone could help Megan, it would be Doctor Telford. He had delivered both her and Megan. Even though he proclaimed himself, "just a doctor for country folks," her mother bragged on him, saying he moved to Dover to get away from the big city life. She, herself, loved him because of his kindness, his smiling eyes, and comforting, reassuring voice.

Nhaya searched the west hall for her mother. A nurse in a white cap and coat from behind the center desk finally raised her head after Nhaya had passed by her twice. "Can I help you, miss?"

"I'm looking for Megan Winters. She was brought here a little while ago."

The nurse looked down, checking her files. "She's in room 222, down the other side and through the double doors."

"Thank you," Nhaya spoke quietly. When Nhaya entered the room, Megan's eyes were closed. At first glance she thought she might be dead. Nhaya fell into her mother's arms. "Oh, Mom, I am so sorry! I had to come." Nhaya clung to her.

"How did you get here stunned by her presence? "Did Adam bring you?" She pried Nhaya's grip from her arm and brushed away her wet tangled hair and looked at her face.

Nhaya bowed her head and ignored the question. "I have something terrible to tell you." Her voice trembled as her tears threatened to fall. Before she could change her mind, she blurted it out, "Megan ate a mushroom tonight that might be poisonous."

"She did what?" Her mother pulled Nhaya out of the room and into the hallway. "Talk to me. How could you possibly know such a thing?"

"Because—because Megan got into my room and rummaged through my stuff!" Nhaya voice raised. I found some special mushrooms I brought back. You know how nosey Megan is…" her voice trailed off.

"Mushrooms? Where did you get mushrooms?"

"I picked them in the mountains and brought them home." Nhaya waited.

"What did I hear?" Doctor Telford asked, walking up behind them.

For a moment, he was silent and then wrote something down on Megan's chart. Removing his glasses, his bushy eyebrows became fixed in a frown as he cleared his throat. Speaking in a serious voice, he said, "Let's all step into the office next door."

The doctor sat down beside Nhaya. "Now," the doctor said after composing himself, "tell me all you know, Nhaya."

"Megan ate a mushroom that Nhaya found in the woods at camp," her mother answered for her.

"Did you pick them yourself, Nhaya?"

"Yes. I found them on a nature walk. I brought them back for my friend's botany class." Nhaya looked at her mother. Tears welled up. "I had no idea they were poisonous, honest." Nhaya's voice wavered. "I would never do anything to hurt my sister!"

The doctor rested his hand on Nhaya's knee. "Of course, you wouldn't."

Miriam continued to pull tissue from the box next to her chair.

"That would explain some of her symptoms," the doctor slowly nodding his head. "Megan is showing signs of food poisoning—muscle cramps, sweats, high fever, and diarrhea, but they shouldn't have manifested for several hours, somewhat a-typical."

The doctor scratched his head. "Okay. "Nhaya, do you know the kind of mushroom she ate?"

"Let's start there."

"No." She brushed the never-ending flow of tears back with her sleeve. "I know she didn't eat a whole mushroom. She left some."

"Well, that's good news." The doctor retrieved another box of tissues and handed it to Nhaya. "Now we have something to go on. How long ago did she eat this mushroom?" He looked at Miriam.

Miriam lifted her arm to read her watch. "Sometime after three and before five."

"That helps me."

"Then she'll be, okay?" Miriam questioned him.

"Most mushrooms that grow in the Pacific Northwest are poisonous, and ninety-nine percent of them are deadly. I have to know what I am dealing with here before I can assure you of anything." The doctor turned and grabbed a huge medical book from behind him on a shelf and began thumbing through its worn pages.

Nhaya felt the cold stare from her mother. She looked up at her for reassurance but found none.

"There are four stages to most mushroom poisonings. It usually takes 6 to 24 hours before the first symptoms occur. After two to three days of severe illness, a day of remission occurs. Then if, and I say if, the mushroom turns out to be deadly, that's when the real trouble starts." Doctor Telford closed the book. "Because we have caught this early, we will try to dilute the toxins in her stomach before they damage her organs. After getting that species, we will know what to expect and act on it."

"Then she'll be all right?" Nhaya wiped fresh tears.

"I have to be honest with you both. We won't know anything for at least twenty-four hours. It all depends on what kind of mushroom she ingested. Some are worse than others. Morels are plentiful in Idaho and not quite as pesky." Doctor Telford smiled. "Let's hope she ate one of those. Her symptoms fit morel poisoning better than anything else right now."

Nhaya's fears were replaced with hope along with a little color to her cheeks. She had remembered collecting morels. They were larger and meaty.

"And if not…" Miriam looked up; she was still as white as a sheet.

"Let's not go there right now, Mom," Nhaya pleaded. "She will be okay."

"Nhaya is right. Let's not borrow trouble."

"I need to know everything," Miriam said flatly. "I can't go through another death without knowing what I am up against."

"Then I'll try to be frank, Miriam. We are not set up for medical emergencies of this capacity. If she should go into renal or liver failure, we'll have to life-flight her to a larger hospital. We should blood-type you both as donors if she needs a kidney transplant. I'll make all the necessary arrangements. First things first. Now, can you get home fast and bring that mushroom back here, Nhaya?"

"Yes."

Doctor Telford stood up. He wrapped a comforting arm around Miriam. "I'm so sorry, Miriam. You have had a lot to bear. Two tragedies shouldn't happen to any one family, so I'm going to see it doesn't. You can stay in here, Miriam. There is water and cups on my desk. Feel free to use the private bathroom to freshen up. Now, if you will excuse me, I have some work to do." The doctor took the chart and pushed the door open with his elbow like a scrubbed surgeon would on his way to the O.R.

"Where's Adam?" Miriam looked down the hall. "Can he take you home and bring you right back?" Miriam collapsed onto the sofa.

"He didn't bring me, Mom."

"Are you with Monica?" Miriam blew her nose. Her face was swollen from crying.

Nhaya stood with her hands behind her back like a small child trying to hide something. Another fib wouldn't hurt. Her mother had given her a good alibi by bringing up Monica. Right now, she would do anything to avoid adding more pain to her.

Nhaya's hesitance warned Miriam. Miriam gave Nhaya the "it better be believable" look.

Nhaya sighed. "No, I drove here."

"You drove what?"

"Your car."

"The DeSoto—without a license? You can barely drive, Nhaya. What on this earth possesses you to do the things you do?" Miriam walked outside the office and looked out a window in the hallway. The storm was still raging. "You could have been in an accident, and then I wouldn't have any children."

"I did okay."

"You did okay! Don't you think? How could you have left something so harmful just lying around the house?" Miriam's voice was growing louder by the minute.

"I didn't just leave them lying around." Nhaya's face burned hot. "I said they were in MY room, in MY backpack!"

Her mother stared at her. "Yes, I hear you, and your sister could die!"

"This isn't my fault." Nhaya dug her fingernails into her tightly fisted hands. "I know it should be me lying there, not Megan. She doesn't give you grief. That is all I do!"

For a moment, Miriam stood speechless. When Nhaya reached the end of the hallway, Miriam had managed to find her voice and called out after her.

Nhaya couldn't hear her mother's cries. The voices inside her head were screaming louder.

CHAPTER FIFTEEN

Nhaya stumbled down the hospital's front steps and fled aimlessly into the street, stinging tears and rain blinding her vision. She heard the screeching followed by a loud blast from a horn.

"Hey! Watch where you're going! Get out of the road."

Nhaya didn't move. *Just run me over and get it over with!*

"Teenagers." She heard as the man drove around her.

Nhaya found herself beside the drugstore two blocks from the hospital. She ducked into the corner phone booth, shaking from the rain. Reaching into her pocket, she grabbed some change for the payphone. The phone rang several times before Monica answered.

"Monica, it's me." Nhaya tried to calm her voice. "What we talked about happened. My sister somehow found the mushrooms."

"You are joking- she didn't eat them - did she?"

"I wish to God I was. She ate part of one. Megan got into my backpack just like I feared." Nhaya spoke in rapid breaths. "I felt something was wrong; but I was too late getting home. She must have been looking for her birthday present. I knew this could happen!"

"Okay, Ny, you're talking too fast again."

109

Nhaya took a deep breath. "Megan's in the hospital, very sick. My mom is at the hospital with her. She practically fainted twice." Nhaya's teeth chattered but not from the cold.

"Nhaya, I don't know what to say."

"My mother went ballistic on me." Nhaya wrapped her jacket tighter around her.

"That's not fair, Ny; you didn't do anything."

"If I hadn't gone to camp, none of this would have happened."

"That's not fair either. You go to camp every year. It's your favorite thing. We can't just stay home in our beds for fear of making mistakes."

"Every summer I went to swimming classes, too." Nhaya bit her lip. She wished she hadn't said it. "My father died because of me."

"Nhaya, please don't go there again. Nothing and no one could have saved your father. It was an accident. Your father was too far gone even before they tried save him. He'd lost too much blood."

Nhaya was silent. "Thank you, Monica. I probably just needed to hear that again. It's just everything is out of control. I took my mother's car too. She left me at home and went in the ambulance." Nhaya looked around. "At least that stupid bird isn't here."

"Bird?"

"I haven't told you. Believe it or not, there's a bird that's been following me since camp. I see it everywhere I go. Now, after this, happened, I'm sure it is and was a bad omen. It was trying to warn me."

Nhaya shook her head as if trying to clear her mind. "It sat on top of the trash can at camp to keep me from taking the mushrooms. I didn't pick up on it until now."

"I'm not following you, Nhaya, why were the mushrooms in the trash?"

"Because Renée ratted on me."

"Boy, I'm missing part of this story. Are you at the hospital? You need to stay there until I find a way to get you."

Nhaya held her hand to plug one ear. "I can't hear you very well, too much noise from the storm and the traffic. I have a way home," she spoke louder. "Can you just meet me at my house and bring your botany book? The hospital needs to know the name of the mushroom she got into. It's still upstairs in Megan's room."

"Yes, I can hear you. I'll find someone to bring me over."

"It's on Megan's nightstand. Please hurry. If I don't get there before you, call the hospital and tell them what kind it is. Talk to my mother or the doctor. He's waiting to hear."

"Hang on, Nhaya; let me get a piece of paper. What's the doctor's name again?"

"T-e-l–f-o-r-d." Nhaya spelled it out. "Our family doctor. The backdoor of my house isn't locked. Did you get all of that?"

"Nhaya, you are really worrying me. What are you going to do now?"

"I don't know yet, but I'll let you know when I find out. Promise."

"You better."

"Thanks, Monica."

Nhaya took another deep breath, What was she going to do now?

The rain pelted her, again, as she ducked her head and crossed the street back toward the hospital. The DeSoto was still parked by the backdoor of the hospital, but a slip of paper in a plastic bag was attached to the car's windshield. She pulled it off.

"A parking ticket! You've got to be kidding me!" Getting into the car, Nhaya shoved the pink slip deep into the glove compartment and slammed it shut.

Sitting at the wheel, Nhaya tried to concentrate. Remembering the lights and the wipers this time, she started the car and shifted into reverse but forgot to look into the rear-view mirror. A horn blasted behind her. She hit the brakes, forgetting the clutch. Her sore ankle screamed in protest. The car lurched and died. Her nerves where shot. She just wanted to lie down, even if for only a few minutes.

Glancing behind her, Nhaya started the car again. She felt the pain surge in her ankle and wished she had taken the time to find the aspirin bottle her mother kept in the car before she had gotten on the road.

The engine began to sputter. She looked nervously at the panel of lights on the dashboard. The fuel gage read almost empty. It would be just a matter of time before she ran out of gas. She hit the steering wheel with both hands.

"Can't you keep gas in your own car, Mother?"

The car rolled to its final stop three miles from home. Stepping out into the road, she raised the trunk, looking for one of her mother's umbrellas. She was prepared for everything. It wasn't strange to see duct tape, hairspray, and hair cutting scissors all in the same box.

She held the umbrella over her already soaked head and prayed silently. "Please protect this car from anything happening to it. It's all my mother has."

The rain bounced hard on the pavement. She limped on one foot down the side of the road, pacing herself for the miles. She thought the day would never come when she would regret going to camp. It was because of Monica she had broken the rules and collected the mushrooms.

Monica was always looking for ways to get extra credit for her classes. She just wanted to do something nice for her.

Could she have seen the signs? She didn't see any of them. Renée's scolding could have actually been a warning. Once again, her father's words came to her: *Sometimes the Great Mystery is offering us help. Pay attention. Wisdom comes from the Great Spirit. If something seems wrong, it probably is.*

Right or wrong, would she have paid attention to Renée, of all people? The bird not moving from the trash lid should have been a huge one for her, even if the bird had no clue what it was doing. If she'd stayed home instead of sneaking out, Megan's curiosity wouldn't have been tested.

Nhaya shook her head; and sighed heavy with regrets.

A heavy gust of wind snapped the umbrella turning it inside out. Heavy rain lashed at her unprotected face. She let go of it and watched it tumble down the highway.

Nhaya covered most of her face with her jacket as she noted the familiar trees that lined the deserted country road. The big elms helped give her a sense of how far she had come. She had counted those trees many times to pass the time when she rode by them with her mother, Judging by the large oak across the field, it would take her another half hour to get home.

Helpless, hopeless, and exhausted, she knelt and quietly hung her head. "Please, help me!" She didn't have the strength to say more.

A ray of hope, like a rainbow breaking through the darkness, brought the woman in her dream to mind. The Indian woman that beckoned to her from camp. Now the woman's words in the dream became clear: "You saw me and you will come." She needed to get back to camp. Someone had to find her. Nhaya was sure the woman's people had been sick by eating many things like bad roots and herbs, including mushrooms. "That was her answer!" *Follow the signs.*

Nhaya lifted her head. "Thank you," she whispered. Thank you.

CHAPTER SIXTEEN

Things were turning around. Headlights approached her and she hoped for a ride. Nhaya shielded her eyes from the bright lights as the brown Chevy station wagon pulled up beside her, and the driver rolled down his window.

"Need a ride?" His smile seemed fake.

"Damien? What on earth are you doing out here?"

"I should ask you the same question. Get in you are soaking wet.

Nhaya thought twice about accepting a ride. but she slid into the worn fabric seat. Her tennis shoes soaked the rubber mat on the floorboard. "How did you know where I was?"

"What makes you think I was looking for you?"

She felt the embarrassment again with her assumption.

"Here, put this on." He offered her his sweatshirt.

Grateful, Nhaya shed her jacket.

Damien's eyes weren't on the road. The outline of the necklace showed through her thin cotton blouse. "How was camp? I didn't see you again."

"I didn't see you either." Her voice was a shiver.

"Were you looking for me?" Damien smiled.

"No, not really." Trapped again. His questions always made her feel the need to explain herself. She wrapped the warm sweatshirt closer around her shoulders. "So, where were you going?"

"Up north," Damien said. "Why are you running around out here in this weather?"

"I was going to the bus station. My car ran out of gas." "You are picking up someone?"

"Just a friend." Nhaya gave him a half-truth. She intended to recruit Adam.

"Must be a guy."

"Why do you say that?"

Damien gave no response. He glanced toward her.

What must he think of her? She was soaking wet, accepting a ride with a guy she barely knew. Was this an accident that their paths crossed again. Read the signs.

"So what tribe are you from?" Nhaya turned toward him and began a friendly conversation.

"I'm Sioux. I was born in Kalispell, Montana, but our clan comes from the Great Plains."

That was how he knew about her bow. The special wood came from his tribal area. "Are you here on vacation?"

Damien laughed. "You don't get around much, do you? How old are you anyway, nineteen?"

"Almost seventeen."

Nhaya glanced in the back. There were several empty whisky bottles lying on the seat. A handgun prodded from a duffle bag which was partially covered by a worn blanket. His bow was also carefully covered by a bag made of leather.

"Seventeen," Damien repeated. "I'm robbing the cradle. I've been on my own since I was twelve."

"Oh. where are your parents?"

Damien smiled, "Probably dead."

"I'm sorry," Nhaya apologized.

"Don't be. I'm not. by the way the gun back there is for safety." Damien glanced back in his rearview mirror. "Can't be too careful these days; don't you agree?" Damien looked at her in a way she didn't understand.

Her father hadn't owned a gun. If he wanted to hunt, he would take his bow and knife. It was the last thing she expected Damien to have. She was about to tell him of the loss of her father, then thought better of it. "So where are you going?"

"Wherever adventure takes me."

"I have an aunt that lives in Montana," Nhaya said. "I'm going up to stay there next summer." Nhaya wanted to keep the conversation light. She was grateful Damien had been driving by on the same road she was on, but at the same time, it seemed hard to believe it was just by accident. The thought awakened her senses.

"It's a great drive; we can go up there together," Damien commented.

"Now?"

"Why not? Unless you have something important to do."

"I do." Nhaya paused. "I have something very important to do." Nhaya glanced at her watch.

"Seems everyone is in a hurry." Damien stretched in his seat and then pulled out a cigarette from his shirt pocket. "Mind if I smoke?" His thumb pushed the black knob on his dashboard. He cracked his window open enough for the smoke to escape the moving car.

"We are only fifteen minutes away from the station now."

"Thanks." Nhaya spoke with appreciation. She thought about telling Damien her predicament. He could possibly help her. She really needed someone like him to reassure her she was on the right track. Then she sighed. Did she actually know him? Her answer was no. She dismissed the thought.

"Not many people are here tonight." Damien observed when he pulled into the bus station parking lot. "This storm must have kept most people from traveling, except for the brave." He looked at her as if expecting an answer.

He couldn't possibly know anything. She felt compelled again to tell him something. "A bus ride should be safe," was all she said.

Nhaya remembered Adam's car and how its powerful motor sounded as they drove away from the station earlier. Damien's station wagon sounded like it was on its last leg as he pulled in. Earlier, she had thought of asking Damien to take her back to Cocolalla, but after she discovered he had a gun, she decided not. Did he know something that she didn't? Maybe the bus would be canceled.

Damien picked a spot close to the front that was sheltered from the rain and turned the key off. The engine sputtered and coughed before it died. Damien smiled sheepishly. "It needs a little work."

Nhaya was anxious to call Monica. "You don't need to come in." She smiled and handed him his sweatshirt.

"I don't mind. Let's grab some coffee and chat awhile— take the chill off."

Nhaya looked at Damien and for once his smile was sincere. It touched her. She had always been a sucker for a clean-cut guy in jeans and a white button-down shirt. And he smelled good, too, from some sort of aftershave. She smelled it when he reached over and handed her his sweatshirt. As she pulled it over her head, the woodsy fragrance lingered on his clothing. She smiled at the thought, because he obviously didn't need aftershave. His native skin couldn't sport a beard.

Nhaya was strangely drawn to him—maybe because they were kindred spirits of the same race. Both were on an adventure and perhaps neither of them by their own choice. She sensed there was much more to Damien, and for a moment, she wished they were in another time and place.

"I really do appreciate the ride, but things are just really complicated for me right now."

"Another guy?"

Nhaya was silent.

Damien looked thoughtful. "Well, my loss. I will find you again. Promise."

Nhaya studied his face. He was a different person than she met at camp. He was still arrogant but then kind. He teased her but she liked it. Before Nhaya opened the car door, she asked, "What is your given name? It's not Damien."

"You're right."

"So, tell me." Nhaya grinned.

"My given Sioux name is Matoskah."

"What does it mean?"

"That's for another time. Perhaps the next time we meet."

He gave her one of his smiles as she shut the door. and drove away in his station wagon as if he were in a fancy Cadillac. When the low hanging tail pipe hit the street, sparks flew across the asphalt.

Ducking into the bus station's phone booth, Nhaya shoved her change into the phone. Please answer, Monica.

The pickup on the other end was almost immediate. "Thank heavens you are there!" Nhaya exclaimed with relief.

"Where else did you think I'd be? Where are you?"

"I just got to the bus station."

"The Sandpoint bus station? I thought you were coming home."

"Monica, Mom's car ran out of gas outside of town. I had to hitch a ride."

"Hitchhiking! Who with?" Monica gasped. "A guy I met at camp."

"Good grief, girl, I leave you alone for a week and look what happens?" Monica tried to make a joke, but it fell flat. "What are you doing at the bus depot?"

"I'll explain later. The mushroom, did you find it?"

"Yes. Let me open the book to the right page."

Nhaya begged under her breath. "Please, please let it be the morels."

"I'm pretty sure it's either an Amanita phalloides or tiger tricholoma." She stuttered at the pronunciation. "They both look like the piece that's left. Nhaya, I just can't believe I am here doing this!"

"Are you sure it's not a morel? Dr. Telford said morels are the most common in Idaho."

"No, it's a puffball. All mushrooms that are in the puffball category are poisonous."

Nhaya couldn't speak.

"Why did you get a ride to the bus station?"

"I didn't get to tell you this, but I met a medicine woman at camp this week. Well, I kind of met her. I am sure she can help Megan. Remember my dream, Monica; the one where this old Indian woman keeps appearing? I swear the woman in my dream is the same woman I saw at camp. In my dream the woman keeps telling me, "You will come.""

"I don't follow you. You think this woman you saw at camp is still at the campsite? It's too late to go up there now. Wait till morning; we can go together."

"I don't have time to wait, Monica. You know that better than I do. If that mushroom, she ate was poisonous, Doctor Telford said she could have a better chance if caught within twelve hours. After that time, the poisons will begin to affect her organs."

"Can't you call the lodge to find her?" Monica suggested.

"I wouldn't even know who to ask for."

"How are you going to find her then?"

"I will find her. Will you call the hospital and tell them the name of the mushroom?"

"I'm sorry, Nhaya, you're right. I just can't imagine you trying this alone."

Nhaya searched for Adam among the travelers in the station. It was just her luck that he was working tonight. She spotted him near the restrooms, mopping floors.

"What are you doing here, Nhaya? You're wet and you're shivering." He rubbed her arms trying to warm them.

"I have to get back to Camp Cocolalla, tonight."

"Tonight?"

She pulled him over toward a bench near the back of the room. Adam took off his parka and handed it to her. She clutched it as they sat huddled together in quiet conversation. Adam listened patiently.

The numbness and shock had begun to wear off, and the reality of what she had to do set in. Nhaya rocked back and forth tucking her hands between her knees choosing her words. Adam listened.

"I picked some mushrooms at camp that turned out to be poisonous. Megan got into my bag and ate one while I was with you this afternoon. She is at the hospital extremely sick, maybe even dying."

Adam's coolness disappeared. "You're kidding right? Is this another one of your bird stories?"

"No, Adam." Nhaya pressed the palms of her hands to her eyes."

"How could something like that just happen?"

"I shouldn't have picked them. I knew better. I've got to fix this.

It's my responsibility."

"I knew something was wrong earlier. You know, Nhaya, not everything that goes wrong in your life is your fault. When are you going to get that through your head? Bad things happen to good people all the time."

Nhaya closed her eyes as tears escaped.

"Hey."—Adam lifted her chin—"listen to me. Megan shouldn't have gotten into your personal stuff."

"Adam, she is only six."

He shook his head. "So, talk to me; what's at camp?"

"There was an Indian shaman at camp. I believe she can help Megan."

"You mean a medicine woman like ritual dancing and all that?" Adam said with a half laugh, until he saw the distressed look on Nhaya's face. "What makes you think she can do more than modern medicine?"

"I know it sounds crazy, but there is more to it. I have dreams about this woman. I didn't put two and two together until I saw her at camp, and she spoke to me, telling me to come. It was just like in my dream. She had a medicine bag attached to her walking stick. My father believed in traditional healing, too."

"You mean that mumbo-jumbo stuff?"

"It's not mumbo-jumbo, Adam!"

People turned and stared at her. She lowered her voice. "Many ancient cultures around the world have healing practices that cannot be explained within the parameters of our medicine."

Then, she said something so stupid it ruined all chances of her ever being taken seriously. "I think that bird has something to do with this, too. First, I thought it was a bad omen. Now I think it was trying to help me."

"Not the bird thing again." This time it was Adam's voice that was raised. A lady standing nearby gave him a strange look. Adam took Nhaya's hand and led her back toward the lockers.

"Look"—Nhaya felt compelled to explain the un- explainable again. "The more I've thought about all this, it makes perfect sense. Nhaya began to pace back and forth in front of the lockers, stopping briefly to assure herself she wasn't the only one listening to her analogy. "I believe"—she paused and turned to Adam who stood with his arms crossed—"that the bird has something to do with the old Indian woman. At camp, the mushrooms that I picked somehow got lost. I found them later in the trash in the back of the camp's kitchen. The bird was sitting on the lid.

It wouldn't move until I finally hit it with my trash sack. Then when I left camp, it followed me home like it had a grudge with me." Nhaya took a deep breath. "And that's when I saw it again in my tree."

"So now you think the bird is some kind of messenger sent by the woman to keep you from taking the mushrooms?"

"Yes. That's exactly what I think." She sat down on the bench beside him.

"Is this the kind of stuff you guys believe in?"

"Us guys?" Nhaya stood up. She was tired of explaining herself. Of all people, she was sure Adam would be the one person to believe her. She turned for her last statement. "You said that you knew me. At least that's what you have been saying. Obviously you don't. I need to find a way to get back to camp. I have to find her—"

Adam stopped her short. "Dang it, Nhaya, why do you do these things to me?" He threw his hands up in the air. "You know I can't leave right now. All I am saying is to wait for a few more hours until I can take you." He reached for her as she backed away.

"Don't be angry, Adam." Nhaya voice became soft. "I have to go now—tonight." She had decided Adam's presence was not what she needed. She didn't need to fight or excuse herself for what she believed.

Adam followed her. "This just isn't the best plan." Adam's tone softened. "Just look outside," he begged her. "Look at the sky! This lightning storm could become very dangerous."

Nhaya remembered Damien's remark to her: *"Only for the brave."*

"It's dangerous for Megan right now, too. I need that bus ticket. I only have twelve hours to give Megan a chance to enjoy another birthday."

Adam, worn out from trying to convince her and resolved he couldn't change her mind. "Okay, it's against my better judgment.

At least take my hunting pack. There's a flashlight in it and a few other things you might need."

Opening his personal locker, Adam pulled out a faded green backpack. Reaching into his jeans, he pulled out his wallet. "I'll come up to the camp as soon as I get off work. You call me here immediately when you get to the lodge. They'll transfer the call to me."

"Thank you. I know you don't understand."

"You're right, I don't," Adam said angered. "This is a bad call, Nhaya." He walked with her to the ticket booth and handed the money to the ticket agent. "One ticket to Cocolalla."

"One way or round trip." The man at the ticket booth smiled.

"One way," Adam affirmed. Nhaya stood next to him, silent.

One way. Was that a prophetic word for her? Would she return?"

"That will be fifteen dollars." The attendant exchanged one ticket for the money. "The bus number is 315 and loads in about ten minutes right out these doors." He pointed to the back of the room.

Adam hesitated in handing Nhaya the ticket. "Look, if there is any other way to do this."

"There's not."

What more could she say to him she hadn't already said? He was too angry with her. She wanted to be held and told everything would be all right. Who could she put her trust in now? Where was her security? She was afraid that if she fell into a black hole of fear, she might never return.

A crackled voice sounded from the overhead P.A. system. "Careywood, Hayden, and Cocolalla leaving in five minutes. Please have your ticket stamped before boarding."

As Nhaya boarded the bus, Adam held up his backpack. The door closed behind her. She slipped into a seat and held her hand to the window, but Adam wasn't there. She resigned herself that she was alone again.

Nhaya sat in a daze as the bus began to move. Everything seemed so surreal. Nothing made sense anymore, not even what she was doing now. She shut her eyes tightly and pleaded, *Please, let me just wake up from this nightmare. I want to start this day over again.*

CHAPTER SEVENTEEN

Nhaya moved to a seat closer to the back of the bus. It was nearly empty. She removed Adam's jacket and placed it in the rack above her. The Greyhound bus had far more comforts than the old rickety camp bus; a bathroom, air conditioning, and heat. She made her way to the restroom and slid the "occupied" sign across the narrow door.

After splashing water from the small basin across her face, she examined the smeared eyeliner and matted hair, wondering why she hadn't got more stares. After she returned to her seat, she took off her shoes and curled up for a nap.

Fingering the colored beaded bracelet around her wrist she designed at camp that week, Nhaya thought of the different symbols she could have woven into her bracelet. Nhaya had caught her mother looking at the bracelet in the hospital. Nhaya looked at the symbols she chose again. The words for respect came to mind. She repeated them, "If you cannot show respect, you cannot expect respect." She and her mother had lost respect between them. Nhaya couldn't remember when that had happened? Unconditional love was another choice. Brenda had chosen it. It meant undeserving love—always given—not just when someone felt like it. Had she ever felt that kind of love?

Nhaya's eyes began to close. It would be a long night.

The brakes hissed and the door swung open. "Cocolalla," the bus driver announced. "Hayden, next stop."

Nhaya sat up, her eyes wide awake. She had dozed off! She made her way to the front of the bus, counting her blessings that the rain had finally ended. The bus stopped near the lodge as she had requested. As she stepped down onto the ground, a few drops of rain fell from the trees above, leaving a clean fresh scent of pine in the air. The night's sky burst with stars so clear and bright that they looked like they had been cleaned and polished by the rain and the wind.

Nhaya checked her watch. It was just ten o'clock. This time, as she stepped off the bus, she felt no excitement and noticed something else. She was hesitant. Her self-confidence had taken a giant plunge. Smoke rose from the tall chimney of the two-story log lodge. Other than a pickup parked near the door, there were no other vehicles or campers in the parking lot. She was sure most of the campers had been rained out. It seemed unusually quiet in an eerie sort of way.

"Is someone meeting you here, miss?" The driver called out after her.

Nhaya didn't answer his question. She simply shook her head. She wanted to scream: *"No, I'm here all alone, just looking for an old Indian woman. I don't even know her name, but I'm hoping she will be able to give me a cure for my little sister who is dying because of my stupidity!" Now do you think you can help me?* Instead, her steps were unsure as she hurried into the stillness of the night toward the Cougar Mountain lodge.

Nhaya climbed the uneven wooden steps to the porch landing. Several large wooden rocking chairs had been pulled back and turned over to protect them from the rain. The familiar dented Coke machine stood in the corner, looking as if it had been kicked by various purchasers who had been cheated of their change.

The rustic pine door stood wide open. Nhaya peered through the thin torn screen that barely kept the flies out. Inside, the large rustic lodge was warm and inviting. An elderly man stood behind the bar, his back to her. The banging of the screen door announced her arrival. Turning, the man tilted his spectacles and eyed the newcomer. His face took on a concerned look when he realized the newcomer was a young girl. Then he recognized her face. "It's Nhaya, isn't it? I thought I recognized you. Your dad's Paul Winters."

Nhaya looked closer at the man. "I'm sorry, I don't remember you."

"Spect you wouldn't". The man introduced himself. "My name is Otis. Your dad and I go back a long way. He'd come in here every now and then after hunting to enjoy a beverage. He always brought his wallet out to show me the family. I saw you in the lodge earlier this week with the camp's cook, getting extra supplies."

Nhaya nodded a yes. "We ran out of a few things. Everyone eats more when they go to camp." She found it was easy to talk to him. She understood why her father liked him.

The man picked up his rag and worked as he talked. "Isn't it a little late to be out alone?" He turned away from Nhaya long enough to thread the cleaned glasses onto their holder underneath the counter.

"I'm not alone. Actually, I'm still camping down the road at Cocolalla with…friends." She hoped that answer would satisfy him.

Nhaya glanced around the familiar lodge. It was empty except for two men who were finishing dinner on the restaurant side. The bar side of the lodge was much larger and took on a different look at night. Small candles were lit on the tables; their flickering lights gave it a cozy feel. She regarded the familiar animal heads that hung over the mantle of the stone fireplace. Their glowing faces seem to be saying, *"Come, sit a spell in the warmth of the fire, and we will tell of how we ended up on this wall"*

Nhaya decided to ask. "I'm looking for Joe Eagle Feather, the guide from the Nez Perce tribe. He taught at the camp this last week. Do you know how I can find him?"

Before Otis could answer, a raspy voice rang out from across the room. "I know 'im."

Nhaya moved through the scattered tables toward two men seated in a corner booth. The men appeared to have little interest in her until she asked her question. Nhaya directed her inquiry to the older of the two, a heavyset bald-headed man.

She tried to ignore the second one; the younger man, who wore a dirty orange fishing vest. It wasn't his rumpled appearance that disturbed her, but it was the way he used his small, jagged hunting knife to clean the contents from underneath his fingernails, discarding it on his pants.

Nhaya read the name sown on the younger man's shirt, *Ned*. She also noticed that he seemed to be amused at her distasteful appraisal of him.

Ned guzzled the rest of his beer, slamming the glass down on table, then He licked his lips savoring the very last drop. Nhaya couldn't take her eyes from him.

"The answer to your question," Ned began, "Eagle Feather headed up north this mornin'. I watched 'im leave. He rode with another guy and a younger Indian in a brown Chevy wagon."

Nhaya forced herself to be polite as he spoke in his broken uneducated manner. After he finished, all she could think of to say was, "Thank you."

Turning around, Nhaya began to retrace her steps, then her eye caught a picture on the wall that caused her to stop. Walking over, she touched the frame of the old black and white photo. Why hadn't she noticed this picture before? Her eyes grew wide.

"Actually," she spoke loud enough for all three to hear, "I am really looking for this woman here standing in this photo." Nhaya pointed to the picture on the wall. "Who is she?"

The old black and white photo showed nine men in full Indian dress standing beside the wall of a long building. Her father had called it a "long lodge." Communities lived in them many years ago. An Indian woman in her native dress stood among them. She wore a necklace that was full of animal teeth and she stood holding a long pipe.

"WindWalker?" Otis, who had been eavesdropping stopped wiping the same glass and put down his towel.

"That's her name?" Nhaya exclaimed. "WindWalker? I saw her at the campground this week!"

"Don't think so," Otis said. "That's a bit impossible, honey." He moved from behind the bar and sided up next to Nhaya. He looked at the photo.

"WindWalker." Otis took in a deep breath. "This medicine woman lived a long time ago. There has never been anyone quite like her since." He touched the picture with his bent and wrinkled pointer finger. "She was quite the legend in her time, became a powerful healer. Stories among many Indian tribes still tell about her."

Nhaya knew it had to be her. She removed her pack and sat down in the chair next to the picture. Resting her chin on her hands at the small table, she listened intently to Otis, now seated beside her.

Finally tired of listening to Otis' never ending chatter, Ned spat a wad of chew on his plate, and the two men strolled over to the bar and each picked up another beer then sauntered over to the fireplace.

In the brief time Nhaya spent talking with Otis, she began to feel a kinship. He was the first person in a long time who had known and cared about her father.

"You know," Otis said, "it has been told that down through the centuries the Nez Perce, they were the most powerful healers in the Northwest. The reason being, they knew how to pass their knowledge to the next tribal shaman found worthy, making each new shaman greater than the last. WindWalker was the last of her bloodline, and her healings were beyond anything that has ever been."

Otis rubbed his stubbled chin. "Legend has it that WindWalker could harness the wind, even dry up a riverbed to where there was nothing left but dry fish bones. Their stories also told that she could talk to the animals. And her prayers, they were very powerful. Once, her ceremony kept a man from death by reaching out and yanking the man's spirit back from the hereafter!" His hand made a yanking motion. Nhaya's mouth fell open in shock. She knew this woman could heal Megan, there was no doubt in her mind!

"See that pipe she's holding there?" Otis looked at the picture again. "That is the ceremonial pipe they used in their ritual healings."

Nhaya examined the picture. It looked just like the pipe the woman at camp was holding. Her excitement grew as Otis settled in for more conversation.

Pulling out his own small pipe, he knocked the stale tobacco from it, replacing it with new.

"See those carvings on the stem? They represent everything growing on the earth. At the end of the long stem is the bowl of the pipe which symbolizes the flesh and blood of their people. When smoke rises from the bowl, it represents the breath of the prayers from the people going up to Wakan Tanka. That's one of the American Indian names to describe our God." He finished in way of explanation.

"How do you know so much about the ceremonies?" Nhaya interrupted. "They are sacred."

"Well,"—he laughed— "mostly through stories from people who have passed through here. Being a barkeeper and all, you hear a lot of things."

"I didn't mean to interrupt," Nhaya apologized. "Please continue about the ceremony; is there anymore?"

"Oh, the rest of the ceremony, yes, their prayers would bring health and blessings to the people in their tribe. To be honest, I'm surprised that I actually recall so much of it." He laughed. "I don't get to tell it very often. People from these parts of Northern Idaho and Montana know lots of stories about WindWalker and the famous Nez Perce Nation. The Nez Perce were a very friendly and peaceful people. Your history book also tells how helpful the Nez Perce were in getting Lewis and Clark through the mountains of Idaho in the winter months. They fed them and sheltered them too. Did your father tell you that in the 1830s the Nez Perce tribe had the first American Bible written in their language? It was the book of Matthew."

"No, he didn't," Nhaya said amazed.

"It's in a museum now in Spalding, Idaho, but my favorite story didn't come from any history book. It came from a man who had passed through here several years ago." Otis set his pipe aside, giving the story his full attention. "It was late one night and we got to talking. The man told me an amazing story. He said centuries ago his ancestors' holy man and the tribe were often visited by a man in a white robe. It could have been an angel; they have presented themselves to many ordinary people that way, you know." He cleared his throat. "Over the years I have become less closed minded about such things."

Otis watched the men by the fireplace. He chuckled again and pointed at the two men seated by the fire. "Every time I talk about how the Nez Perce had a copy of the Bible written in their own language and could have been visited by angels, those two guys move as far away from me as they can."

Otis laughed out loud. "Lord, forgive me. So, this person helped their people. He talked of many herbs and roots that had healing properties for their people. Some of which aren't even found now.

Nhaya looked at Otis wide-eyed.

"This story I'm about to tell you now is my favorite. It was early spring and time for the Nez Perce to move on and find the bison. Every year they journeyed across a pass from the panhandle of Idaho into Montana. That year the snow had not melted enough to get through. If they went back, starvation would have killed most of the women and children. The elders of the tribe went to their holy woman for help. Their holy woman went away to fast and pray. Within a time, instead of snow, warm rain began to fall, melting the heavy snow that prevented them from crossing. The passage was cleared for the people. The amazing thing was it only rained where they needed to cross."

Like a child, Nhaya began to laugh with pleasure. To her, hearing the stories was like old times.

"My father told me stories of great faith too." Nhaya quickly removed her necklace showing it to Otis. Her eyes sparkled.

"My, my, isn't that something. This yours?

"It was my father's. Do you know anything about it?" Nhaya waited, breathless.

Otis took it and examined the markings. "Can't say I do."

"Oh." Nhaya put it back on.

"But that doesn't mean much. Those markings look to be more like hieroglyphics from Biblical times."

"According to some, there are still sightings of WindWalker. Some believe she had the power to overcome death, so she's never died. But I say if she is still around, she would have to be very old."

Otis was silent for a moment, then he looked in Nhaya eyes. his voice more somber. "Honey, you know that's only a legend.

"How about Lazarus? I learned about him in church camp."

"In the Bible—Lazarus? Yes, Jesus restored Lazarus back to life, but in the end, when his time was up, he died anyway. But you need to consider the part after we leave this earth, too, and where we will be going."

Otis looked at the small gold band on his right pinky finger. "It was my wife's wedding ring. I still wear mine, too."

Nhaya touched his arm. "I'm sorry."

"That's quite all right, honey. I will see her again." He slapped at his knee. "Seems like one memory leads to another."

"How old would she be now?"

"My wife?"

"No, I'm sorry. WindWalker."

"Let's see. I'm near seventy." He scratched at his head. "That would make her in the vicinity of, I'd say, well over 100 years old. So, the woman you are looking for could not be her."

Nhaya picked up her pack, refreshed again. "Thank you for talking to me, Otis. I see how you and my dad became good friends. I better get going." She motioned toward the door. "Could you just point me in the direction where the tribe last camped?"

"The Nez Perce used to camp somewhere over Pine Ridge," he recalled. "That's about ten miles up that mountain as the crow flies. They used to come into town, every once in a while, for supplies."

"You're not planning on going up that mountain tonight, are you?"

"Oh, good heavens no." Nhaya didn't turn around as she walked out the door.

Maybe she was an apparition. All she knew was she saw her at camp. Real or not she would soon find out. "WindWalker," she spoke her name for the first time. *That was her name.*

"WindWalker," she said it again, liking the sound of it. She retraced her path down the steps.

"Hey, missy, sounds like you could use some help." The screen door slammed again and the man in the orange vest stood on the porch. He spat out a spew of tobacco juice wiping his face with his sleeve. "If you need a guide, I can help. I know these woods like the back of my hand."

At first, Nhaya didn't hear Ned's invitation. Her head was swimming with information. She was busy calculating the time she had left.

"Name's Ned." He stepped off the porch and headed in her direction. "Don't know if you caught it. I didn't catch yours. Pretty thing like you shouldn't be alone out here."

Was he joking? "I don't need anything but thank you," Nhaya called out.

"I've been a guide in these parts of the woods," he re-assured her, "and I know where them Indians camp out." Ned continued to walk behind her.

Nhaya could smell the liquor on his breath. She shivered at the stench. Turning around she faced him. His deep-set eyes seemed to enjoy the journey as they traveled up and down her body, coming up to rest on the loosely tied strings of her shirt.

Nhaya reached up and covered the spot with her hand. "Thanks, Ned," she said it again, "But I'm far from being alone. I have my family with me." She continued to walk in the direction of the campgrounds.

"I'll be around if you need me to find that squaw," he called after her. "I know the woods real good."

Nhaya shivered again with distaste. His enjoyment of playing with her was evident. *Know them like the back of his hand.* Adam had said the same thing about her, knowing her like the back of his hand, only it was comforting when he said it. How many times would her luck hold out tonight? She had always felt safe in these woods. She could not let Ned or anyone else intimidate her.

Nhaya passed the dirt turnoff from the highway into Camp Cocolalla. A clump of bushes hid part of the road sign. Before crouching down and unzipping her jeans, she checked for oncoming cars. Funny how it worked. When she was near a bathroom she never needed to go.

Nhaya reasoned with herself about any danger she could encounter. In her self-defense class, she learned the basics. Her father had taught her the element of surprise, but that was for bully's not animals.

It was time now to consider her strategy. She hadn't hiked in the woods for a long time and then only in the daylight. There were several wooded paths that led to Pine Ridge. She had hiked them many times. Her best bet would be the one most traveled, and if the moon gave off enough light tonight, she could make good time. It was getting darker. The moon's glow hidden by the tree line. Her heartbeat quickened as she fixed her eyes on the shadowy unclear darkening path. Somewhere between her, the forest, and its inhabitants was an Indian shaman woman named WindWalker that she badly needed to find.

CHAPTER EIGHTEEN

*N*haya turned around one last time and peered out toward the main road. She waited, listening. Beside her a twig snapped. She looked down in time to see a squirrel scamper up the branch beside her. She relaxed. The hoot of an owl off in the distance were familiar sounds usually present at night in the woods, nothing to alarm her of a present danger, animal or man. Even though, she breathed a sigh of relief; the comfort of familiarity with the forest had changed.

For the first time, she felt unsure of her abilities. In the growing darkness, nothing looked the same. Bushes took shapes and forms. The trees seemed taller, and the foliage over grew parts of the path.

She took a deep breath, shaking off thoughts of failure, and squinted at her watch. Unable to read it, she pulled its face closer to make out the time. A half hour had already passed. The shortcut straight up would cut off time but there was also the fear of getting lost.

Nhaya calculated the time again. From her mother's memories. Doctor Telford's diagnosis hadn't shocked her as much as it had her mother because Monica had already informed her of the tragic fate of those who had eaten them, innocent of their deadliness.

The sooner she got back; the better Megan's odds were. In biology class she learned how scientists would milk poisonous snakes to make anti-venom, and there were shots that could reverse the toxins for allergic reactions of bee stings. Why couldn't medical science find a cure for stupid mushroom poisoning?

Two hours of hiking up the steady incline and she was already exhausted. She hunched down on her sneakers and stared into the forest's inky blackness. Looking up through the tops of the trees, the sky revealed a crisp, clear starlit night, the heavy clouds only a memory. How would she get through the night? She had begun the long journey toward Pine Ridge, placing all her hopes on someone she thought she saw at camp; someone who had talked to her in her dreams, and maybe the same someone she found in an old black and white photo at the lodge of a woman that was much too old to even still be alive.

Nhaya pulled off Adam's pack. Unable to see the inside, she reached in, feeling for the flashlight. The handle was big and bulky and hard to hold with her small hand. She switched it on—saved again by Adam. Being prepared was supposed to be her motto, not his. She fought the sudden urge to cry. She should have made peace with Adam before she left - In case she didn't return. She thought of her father and her words echoed back. *I didn't even get to say goodbye.*

The forest floor was scattered with tree limbs and debris from the storm. Her feet began to hurt from her shoes being damp. She unlaced them and brushed the loose dirt and stickers from her now pukey, shade-of-gray socks. Before she continued, she held the flashlight to her watch. It had been less than two hours since she checked it last.

Nhaya continued her arduous journey. The trail narrowed and the bushes crowded in on the footpath. A rotted tree had fallen, blocking her pathway. Nhaya scrambled quickly over, sliding down the other side. The tough choke cherry bushes jabbed their prickly thorns through her jeans, tearing a hole. Nhaya cried out!

A thorn bit into her flesh. She Knowing the woods beyond would be covered with that bush, she rethought her path.

Nhaya could see the moon now. It had cleared the trees at the top of Pine Ridge. Soon she would start a sharper climb and the trees would thin out, making it easier for her to see by the full light of the moon. Again, Nhaya stopped to listen to the sounds of the forest. Somewhere to her left she could hear the water rushing over the rocks from the crystal-clear creek that she remembered stopping by many times before with her father. Soon the trees would thin out and the trail would be barely visible taking her upward, zigzagging across the mountain's face.

After walking a few yards, the stars suddenly appeared above her in a clear sky. Spread out ahead lay a wildflower meadow filled with delicate yellow flowers. Colors look so different in the moonlight. Nhaya leaned up against the last tree before the clearing, staying out of sight.

Weary, she let go of her guard and sat down. Without thought, she picked up a nearby stick and tossed it. The shrill screech of a barn owl answered the noise as the stick landed.

Nhaya jumped and when the screech came again, she looked above her head. "YOU! What are you trying to do, scare me to death!"

Nhaya couldn't see anything that resembled a camping ground. *This would have been the place,* she shook her head, but there were no signs. No flattened grass and no remnants of a campfire or any evidence of a community. She pulled out the flashlight again and checked her watch. It was after midnight. Otis had told her it was maybe ten miles to where they might be camped if they were still there. It could take her till dawn to reach the top of the mountain. It had been twelve hours since Megan was sick.

Nhaya pulled Adam's pack onto her lap. Tipping the flashlight inside, she searched the contents. Her first encounter was a hard leather object. She pulled out Adam's hunting knife and turned it over, examining the size of the blade without removing it from its sheath. She held it as if she were being attacked. Could she actually stab it into an animal before it got to her?

Her continued search discovered a baggie containing sunflower seeds, a can of a Coke, a book of matches, and a couple of candy bars. Adam always loved Milky Ways. She ate one and then the other. After finishing the Coke, her spirits lifted. Nhaya flipped the flashlight off. Its light had given her comfort but also left her exposed.

Now, she considered the meadow. Crossing in the moonlit would make her even more visible to predators. Anything could be watching her. She had observed small tracks and deer droppings on the sides of the path, but she hadn't seen any obvious signs of cougar tracks, or trees torn by hungry bears searching for insects.

Last week at the lodge café when she had gone with one of the camp cooks to buy extra supplies, she remembered hearing a hunter boast of a cougar he had injured two days before. At that time, sheen visioned the poor cougar lying in some ravine. She now considered the possibility of it still roaming around.

Nhaya stuffed the candy wrappers back in the bag and was about to stand up when a branch snapped. Someone or something was not far behind her on the trail. Nhaya crouched low behind a bush. An animal could have smelled her food. She wanted to kick herself for eating. Maybe it was Ned; the thought of him made her shrink back further into the brush. She hugged Adam's lightweight jacket closer, barely breathing.

It could be the cougar! It wasn't dead, after all, and now it was hungry and stalking her. That caused her to stop breathing entirely. It was either flight or fight, but her legs wouldn't move. Even if she ran across the meadow, she would be taken down like a hunted deer in seconds.

Nhaya reached for the knife. The sound of breaking branches came closer toward her hiding place. She looked down at her jacket. The moonlight made it look like a neon sign!

Nhaya raised the only thing she had at the moment to fend off her attacker—the darkened flashlight. She shut her eyes. Her heart was pounding so fast she wondered if it would burst. Better to die from a heart attack than being torn alive by a mountain lion.

The magnificent animal stood a few feet from her. It was an elk with a rack equal to its height. As it stepped out of the shadows, Nhaya lost her grip on the flashlight and it made a thud when it hit the ground. Startled by the noise, the animal bolted across the meadow.

After her breathing returned to a somewhat normal rhythm, Nhaya hung her head in shame. She gathered up the things from Adam's backpack, angry at herself.

A familiar voice came from the darkness. "You make things difficult for yourself, Nhaya. What's up with your skills? Don't you know braves never go into the woods without a weapon?" He grinned. "Flashlight doesn't count."

She wasn't alone!

Nhaya's eyes darted around looking everywhere. She tried to adjust her vision, peering in one dark place after another at more shapeless forms. "Adam?"

"Nope, but you're lucky I was around. That could have been a grizzly instead of an elk." Damien stepped right in front of her. "The hunter becomes the hunted."

Damien passed his knife back and forth between his hands then holstered it to his hip.

"What?" Damien looked at her in wide-eyed innocence holding up his hands.

"You—you suddenly appear here in front of me again and not invited, I might add. What are you doing up here? And please don't tell me it's a free country again."

"Relax." Damien looked around. "I was just watching your back."

"How did you find me, Damien? Have you been following me all this time?"

Nhaya grabbed Adam's backpack. She couldn't believe his nerve! Had she been that naive or that foolish to think she was safe in these woods at night just because she had hiked there in the day?

"Told you I would be seeing you again." Damien set his bow down.

"This isn't reassuring." Nhaya squared her shoulders and faced him.

"Well, I'm here now. Let's just make the best of it."

She couldn't believe his arrogance. "How can you help me? "I don't need an escort. You can go home now."

"Look, I know who you're looking for. At first, I thought you were just a nut job, but now I understand. So, let's get on with the search."

"What do you mean, 'you know'?" Nhaya demanded. "Just what do you know about me? Why are you really up here?"

"Whoa, hold on there. I came to help you, not be interrogated."

"Help me, how? Just answer the question."

Damien picked up his bow and began to march across the meadow. Nhaya grabbed her pack and quickly passed him by. Damien picked up his speed. When they reached the other side together, both were at a dead run. Nhaya fell to her knees out of breath.

"Come on, Nhaya," Damien panted. "Don't be such a stick in the mud," he teased. "You can't run away from me. Besides, I wouldn't mind meeting the old gal myself."

"The old gal! How do you know about her? If this woman is still alive, she should be treated with the deepest respect," Nhaya snapped.

"Lighten up. I didn't mean anything by it. Look, I'm sorry we got off on the wrong foot. This time I'll take the blame."

"How do you know about her?"

"From Otis, same as you. I stopped in right after you left the lodge."

"You asked him about me?" her face turned red.

"Not exactly. I just told him we were family. He spilled the rest."

"Okay, Damien, Otis didn't know anything. Why do you think I'm looking for her?"

"Well, your girlfriend told me."

"Monica told you about my sister. You went to my house? I don't believe this!

"I sensed you were holding back something. When you jumped on the bus alone, I thought it a good idea to talk to your mother. So yes, I went to your house." Nhaya was aghast "You know where I live?" Nhaya was finally speechless.

"It's not hard to find out where anyone lives, Missy. Isn't that a little beside the point right now?" he said, side-stepping the question.

Nhaya sat down and tried to digest what she just heard. Apparently, he was either a stalker or someone awfully board with life. She hoped he was the second. "What all did Monica tell you?" Nhaya asked plainly.

"That you are on some sort of timeline."

"And…?"

"And that you are looking for someone. I'm assuming it's WindWalker."

"Then you know I don't have much time left before it's too late to help my sister."

Damien held his hand up in front of Nhaya. He reached out and took a hold of the rawhide string that held her father's necklace. "If she's around, you'll find her with this."

Nhaya's face paled. What did he really want, and why was he there?

CHAPTER NINETEEN

In front of them, a small horse trail led from the meadow and disappeared in the middle of a narrow shale ledge. Nhaya pulled off her pack and looked down; the moon's light allowing her to see into its depth.

Damien whistled. "It must be over fifty feet to the bottom." Nhaya's hands turned clammy. She hated heights.

"You really going to cross that?"

"I have no choice." She glanced over the edge. If she fell, she would end up at the bottom of the ravine.

"There is another trail a few miles back," Damien offered. "They all lead the same direction."

"I don't have time to go back."

"Okay, Damien smiled. "After you."

Nhaya glared at him. She emptied Adam's pack, keeping the knife and a few lightweight things. Gingerly, she stepped one foot forward on the faded trail; the other foot remained on solid ground. She swallowed. Taking her second step, she pressed the sides of her tennis shoes deep into the rocky earth, sending pieces of shale rock plummeting to the gully below. She glanced back at Damien for reassurance. When she took the next step, her foot slipped a little further down the mountain, causing her to catch her breath and leaned further back against the side of the cliff face.

A few plants grew from the mountainside. She reached up grabbing some of the roots hoping it would at least steady her.

Fear gripped her when she realized she was still sliding with every step.

The sudden urge to look down overtook her logic. As she turned her foot, to go back, Nhaya dropped to her knees, her hair cascaded over her face. Nhaya stared down the embankment. Trying to stand again, a shower of pebbles beneath her feet began racing away into the darkness below.

"I'm slipping!"

From out of nowhere, a sudden gust of wind came up the valley's floor and pressed her against the mountain's side like a hand holding her steady. Nhaya stood and continued along the ledge until she felt the safety of the ground beneath her feet. The wind stopped as suddenly as it came up.

"Impossible," she whispered, but the wind had held her safe. Nhaya just looked at Damien. She could tell he was grinning. Then he gave her a thumbs up.

"So, are you coming?" Nhaya called back to Damien.

"Who me? The wind doesn't obey me. I don't have the necklace. I'll take the other path."

She wondered at his words, and she wondered if she would wake up soon.

Seeing Damien walk away from her was a huge relief. He hadn't lifted a finger to help her. Had he wanted her to fall? Or maybe he believed she wouldn't. It was the sudden gale of wind. Had it not come up, she would have fallen to her death. She grasped the necklace. Did Damien really believe the necklace was the reason she hadn't fallen? All she knew was that she was being protected.

It was after three a.m., and Nhaya began to worry again. For the past two hours there had been no signs of campfires. The mountainside was sparse of foliage; She hoped the coyotes crying in the distance would remain there, in the distance.

Nhaya's eyes felt like sandpaper and she had developed a throbbing headache. Nhaya rummaged through Adam's pack again hoping she had missed the aspirin. She took out his compass, opening and then closing it again. It seemed useless. There were no more trails. The only direction to go was up.

She knelt on one knee and picked up a smooth stone rubbing it around in her hand with her fingers; a habit acquired from her father when they were hiking. She looked around.

"What should I do?" she said. Although she was unsure to whom she spoke to.

It seemed useless to continue. Even if she did find the camp, would the people help her? And how could she possibly get back in time. She only had a few hours left.

The crushing truth settled on her. It was over. Megan was going to die and there was nothing she could do about it. She bowed her head in defeat, tears spilled down her cheeks.

It was the unmistakable cat's cry that stopped her sobs with a choke. She listened, barely breathing. Was the sound coming from behind her or above?

Most trackers that hunted in these mountains carried a rifle. They came for the trophies. Others just carried a revolver for safety. She had neither. Nhaya brought the pack to her side. Without looking inside. her hand found its target. She wrapped her fingers around the handle of the knife.

Slowly setting the pack down, she squatted and inched herself around like a warrior preparing for battle. Her eyes squinted in the dark, searching for anything moving.

The only time Nhaya had seen a cougar was at the zoo. Now, from across the rocks standing on a fallen log, she faced one of the most beautiful and dangerous of Idaho's alpha predators. Her hand shaking, she unsnapped the strap and pulled the knife free from its sheath. Her stance held strong as she raised the blade, preparing to fight.

The mountain cat moved cautiously toward her as if deciding its next move. She could tell it was wounded. The big cat's yellow eyes tracked Nhaya as she inched toward it. Its piercing cry and uplifted paw told her not to move closer.

Now she knew this was her only chance. She had to be the aggressor. She raised the knife and lunged at the cat, letting out a scream. The cougar backed up and turned away, disappearing into the brush. Nhaya stood her ground and waited for the mountain lion's response. It didn't return.

Trembling, Nhaya dropped the knife and stepped backward. Hysterics and laughter replaced her sobs until she collapsed in a heap on the cold ground. Before losing consciousness, her last thought was of Damien and his offered protection. What would Damien have done if he had been here? Probably wet his pants.

The night's temperatures were coldest before dawn.

Shivering, Nhaya clutched at Adam's jacket and drew herself up beside a fallen tree she wrapped Adam's jacket closer. For a moment, she heard the familiar sound of crickets chirping their night song, and she was home lying on the front swing. Something brought her back to consciousness.

Nhaya wiped her sleeve across her dirty tear-streaked face. She thought about making a fire. There were matches in Adam's backpack. She couldn't sit there for long but a little bit of shelter sounded comforting, and her eye lids were so heavy. She closed them and began to quietly hum the song her father sang to her when she was four. He called it "The Moon Song."

It took a moment to believe her eyes. Keeping them partially shut, Nhaya watched as the hawk peck at her knee. Then it stretched out its large, feathered wings and hopped to a rock beside her.

"What are you doing here?" She eyed the bird as it cocked its head and leapt into flight. "Hey" — Nhaya raised her hand — "I'm sorry, don't leave me here alone. I'm sorry, please, come back!"

Nhaya rallied. She stood up and stumbled across the rocky terrain, desperate to keep the bird in sight. "Wait!" Nhaya yelled breathlessly as the bird glided up and out of her view.

CHAPTER TWENTY

$\mathcal{N}$haya's legs wobbled like jelly as she climbed the last few feet to the plateau. She tossed Adam's backpack aside and stretched out. The Eastern sky began to glow with rich hues of pink and gold.

Nhaya gazed at the picture- perfect view in front of her. A variety of wildflowers popped their heads above the patches of frost. Beyond the colorful meadow of yellow buttercups and sprigs of purple mountain mallow, a long row of lodgepole pines stood like obedient soldiers guarding their forest any further from intruders. A snow-capped mountain jutted out from behind the plateau of trees She could hear a small brook from within the tree line and became aware of her thirst. Nhaya raised her backpack above her head and ran through the wet meadow grass falling down at the brook's edge. She knelt, splashing water across her face. Dipping her bared feet into the stream, she gasped after her brain registered the burning iciness of the water.

Nhaya stayed close beside the stream. Just for a moment, she forgot her grief. She felt peace, and then a presence. Turning around she saw a figure walking toward her.

As the woman drew nearer, Nhaya could see it was an Indian woman! She was clothed like the person she'd seen at camp. A long woolen skirt with animal tails hung from the hem. Her broad shoulders were covered with a purple shawl. The woman's silver hair shone in the morning light. As she came closer, Nhaya studied the lines of age etched in the woman's leathered skin. She knew that the woman in the picture at the lodge and the woman that stood before her were one in the same. The woman called WindWalker.

Nhaya rose, feeling goose bumps on her arms.

"You are real." Nhaya blurted out. "And you are the same woman in my dreams!"

WindWalker turned and pointed her walking stick back in the direction from which she had come. She motioned for Nhaya to follow.

Nhaya picked up her shoes and fell in behind her.

The woman remained silent, and Nhaya wondered if she only spoke the Nez Perce language. She had questions that needed answers. If WindWalker didn't understand her, how could they communicate?

"Do you understand me?" Nhaya spoke again.

WindWalker remained silent and continued to walk the horse trail through the meadow. In a small clearing, not far into the tree line, a small campfire burned just outside a tepee. Nhaya looked around. Was she dreaming?

Nhaya moved close to the fire and rubbed her hands together briskly over the flames. The dull chill in her bones faded as the warmth of the fire spread.

WindWalker motioned for her to sit. She handed Nhaya a piece of dried meat and a tin of tea. Nhaya bowed in respect, but then remembered it wasn't the Indians that bowed low to each other. Embarrassed, Nhaya took the meal from her. She mouthed the words "Thank you."

Nhaya knew it wasn't polite to stare, but she couldn't take her eyes from the woman. Starving, she bit off a piece of the meat. The texture was a little chewy but flavorful. Without thought of her manners, she devoured her food.

WindWalker sat patiently and seemed to observe her, too.

Finally, Nhaya broke the silence. "I'm here because I need your help." She wiped her hands on her jeans then made some gestures that resembled sign language.

"I know why you are here, child."

"You understand me?"

WindWalker put her fingers to her mouth and then to the sky. "The Great Grandfather Spirit has seen your plight. He has sent me to help you."

Before Nhaya could say more, WindWalker spoke again.

"The spirit of pride travels with you. You must learn to walk the Good Red Road." She motioned again to the sky.

"Two paths together form a north- south road. This is your spiritual path; the one where you will walk in the Spirit's power. Then the day of peace will find you."

Day of peace, what was she talking about? Power; what power?

"Young one, our people's ways were simple. Some of them became foolish. They thirsted for their own power. Their wisdom became foolish. They did not understand their Creator."

Nhaya wasn't sure what WindWalker was talking about. She was here for Megan, not for her own problems. But the idea of peace in her life, she would say, amen.

"A virgin?" WindWalker stated.

Was it a question? "Uh… yes, I am." She became embarrassed not understanding her point. She wasn't about to be selected for a sacrifice. She knew there were cultures who offered up virgins as sacrifices because of their purity.

WindWalker stood. "Virgins have great spiritual power." She beckoned to Nhaya.

"Come. "You must enter the tepee here from on the left"—she pointed—"the northeast side in the circle."

Nhaya nodded her head, taking in everything she saw. The tent was amazing, wrapped in real animal hides. The outside covering stopped a few inches short of the ground. Tall polls were tied together at the top with rope of woven hemp. Nhaya touched the animal hide to the tepee's entrance.

"She stepped inside." The view inside looked far larger than it had appeared from the outside. Several bison hides were spread out on the ground, giving it a homey feel. In the middle of the tepee, smooth rocks were being warmed warm by hot coals. A small kettle hung on a black metal stand beside the circle. The sweet scent of lavender filled the air. Overwhelmed by the moment, tears began filling Nhaya's eyes. She tried to blink them back. This had to be a dream.

WindWalker followed her into the teepee and stood opposite of her. She started by hitting her stick on the ground in brisk short taps. "You must enter the healing circle of life." WindWalker drew a large circle around the rocks she placed on the ground.

"Sit here." She pointed.

Nhaya sat cross legged within the circle.

WindWalker moved to the black pot that hung on the stand near the fire and lifted out a wooden cup. She brought it up to Nhaya's mouth. "Drink."

WindWalker lifted her hands to the sky and spoke: "From understanding can come healing."

Nhaya listened as WindWalker began to beat a steady rhythm on the drum, chanting in a rhythmic and compelling tempo. It was like the braves that danced at camp. "Hey-a-ya'- hey, Hey-a-ya'-hey." WindWalker repeated the words over and over.

Nhaya couldn't help but notice the long ceremonial pipe propped up beside the kettle. She recognized it as the one used in healing ceremonies. It was the same pipe in the picture at the lodge. Seeing the pipe sent a thrill through her.

WindWalker continued to chant and dance in the ceremony. Then her steady hands gently lifted the ceremonial pipe up high. Raising her voice, she called out to the sky.

"Great Grandfather Spirit, you have always been. And no other has been. There is no other to pray to but you. Everything that I see has been made by You. The four quarters of the earth You have finished." She pointed to two different places within the circle. "You decide when your glory comes up and when it leaves the earth. Great Grandfather Spirit, lean close to the earth that You may hear the voice I send. To you and all your power, I send a voice for help. The two-legs on earth is in despair." She pointed toward Nhaya.

"For her, I send my voice to You. You have said the weak shall walk. Through Your power with our prayers shall the feeble walk upright."

WindWalker turned around and looked at Nhaya. "From where we are facing, behold a virgin. Look upon the faces of your children that they may also walk the Good Red Road to the day of quiet. This is also our prayer." WindWalker lit the pipe.

Nhaya bowed her head and prayed, too. She remembered her father's words. When two or more pray together, their prayers are stronger, like strings that intertwine make a rope stronger.

WindWalker held the pipe high in the air as the pipe's smoke rose, finding its way out through the opening in the top of the tepee.

Nhaya smiled as she remembered Otis's words. "The smoke is symbolic of prayers of the people, together, rising toward heaven."

Then WindWalker took something from another pot and raised her hands, again, thanking the Great Grandfather Spirit for giving the herbs of the earth that would help heal the young one.

Nhaya watched as WindWalker placed the contents in what looked like an animal skin and tied it with the same material. It was like to the pouch that had been tied to WindWalker's walking stick in Nhaya's dream.

Then WindWalker took four hot rocks from the circle and spoke out: "I pray to You, Great Wind of the Spirit. Hear me." WindWalker placed one of the hot stones behind Nhaya. "Of the north we gain patience and purity. We thank You for these gifts." She walked over and touched Nhaya on the left shoulder. Then WindWalker faced eastward and placed another hot stone on the ground, this time touching Nhaya's right shoulder.

Every time WindWalker touched her, Nhaya felt different inside. WindWalker moved to the south praying the same prayer as before, only asking for discipline and direction instead of patience and purity, placing a stone in front of Nhaya, and finally facing westward.

Each time a hot rock was set in a place and an herbal potion was poured out on it, causing a pungent aroma. Nhaya recognized a couple of the scents. They were sage and cedar.

Nhaya bowed. She began to feel convicted about her attitude; the lies she had told lately, and the way she disobeyed her mother for the sake of her own desires. Ashamed, she whispered, "Forgive me, Great Grandfather Spirit. I have been selfish and mean, and foolish. I have forgotten to pray and hurt my mother by saying things I shouldn't have."

It was the first time she realized how far away she had strayed from her values. An awakening flowed through her. She suddenly wanted to cry out because of all the bad that had happened and let go of her anger fueled by her sense of loss. Then a sweet song sang in her heart. The anguish, sadness, and shame left her and was replaced by peace and a sense of belonging. She wiped away the healing tears that streamed down her face, embarrassed by her show of emotions. Finally, WindWalker stood in the center of the circle with her. "This is where the source of all life and the beginning of the Good Red Road begins."

Nhaya looked around, expecting to see a path beginning at her feet. She rose up and gratefully accepted the bag that WindWalker held out to her. She looked into WindWalker's gentle eyes. They were shining with tears.

WindWalker put her old hands around Nhaya's young ones. "Medicine roots have good healing powers."

Nhaya held on to WindWalker's hands, not wanting to let go. Even if neither had spoken again, everything had been understood. Outside the tepee, Nhaya looked at her watch in the morning light. She tucked the bag into her jean pocket. Then impulsively, she threw her arms around the old woman.

"The Great Spirit tells me about a man with a dark soul searches for you."

"How do you know this?" Nhaya gasped.

"There are good spirits and bad spirits. I have been told this: We do not war against flesh and blood, but spirits of darkness. Some of our people have given themselves over to evil spirits. Heyoka's can do evil. They can give and take away health and use their power for bad. Only a few are left. Most have been driven away from our lands."

Nhaya mentally took a step backward. She hadn't realized that anyone was looking for her. She immediately thought of Ned. He didn't seem evil, just a drunk. "I will be careful." she promised. "May I ask one more thing? Who is this Great Spirit you pray to?"

WindWalker smiled. "Our people have worshiped the one true God for centuries. This is the sign given to our ancestors, the one you wear. The sign bears His name. He is the One who has made the heavens and the earth."

"Nimiipuu, walk the Good Red Road as I have." WindWalker's hand was firm on Nhaya's shoulder.

"Will I ever see you again?"

"As you are one with the Great Spirit, we will be together. The Great Spirit who kept you on the mountain will walk with you until the day of quiet."

CHAPTER TWENTY-ONE

*B*efore Nhaya descended the mountain, she looked back once more, but WindWalker was gone. She smiled and reached for the small leather pouch tucked deep inside her pocket. She must still have a chance to make it back in time.

Her steps were swift but cautious as she followed the familiar terrain back down the mountain side. Her body obeyed her steps, but her mind was somewhere else.

How could she possibly explain the things that had happened? If she told Adam, would he ever believe her? The woman in her dreams had a name, and the Great Spirit had been with her on the north face of the cliff as her shield.

There were still unanswered questions. Like her two paths together making a north-south road. If that was her path, then why did WindWalker tell her to also walk the Red Road? Funny, her father had never mentioned a Red Road. She promised to follow it, but what was it, and where did it begin?

The words she had heard so many times in her dream: "The rest you must choose for yourself." She hoped she would know what to choose when the time came, or maybe she had already chosen.

WindWalker had said something else. She told her she was in danger. Ned's name popped up. She dismissed it. Ned was a drunk, not evil. She would take great measures to stay away from him anyway. She would not be so careless this time.

The early morning chill was still in the air. It was surprising to see the meadow was only a few yards away. She had made good time once she discovered another path that led around that nightmare cliff. Her knees ached from the constant pressure of walking down the steep decline. Stopping to catch her breath, Nhaya stooped and peered through the low branches and shrubs, careful before bursting out onto the meadow. She hadn't seen Damien, but then again, he had snuck up on her more than once already. Maybe he'd just grew tired of playing games.

Nhaya looked back up the trail and sighed. WindWalker was so amazingly...amazing. The old woman had known things; she was gifted.

Nhaya listened to the sound of the brook a few feet away and reasoned that if she stayed off the main path and followed the stream, she would have a better chance of keeping hidden. Nhaya turned from the familiar path and slid down the embankment on her heels, stopping short of the rapidly moving brook.

It was cooler at the water's edge. She bent down to wash her face and hands in the cold water by the rocks. Opening Adam's pack, she retrieved the empty Coke can. Moments later, after gulping her fill of the frigid water, she filled it again, letting the water overflow the can.

She stood and studied the route ahead of her. The brook would eventually turn south again and would force her to leave its safety and climb back up to the trail. She sighed, gathered her resolve, and moved out along the water's edge, scampering over rocks and beneath overhangs in an effort to remain unseen.

Eventually, the water began heading toward the south and the time came to leave its safety, As the sun crested the peak, morning light began to grow on the mountain side and with it came a measure of confidence as the forest resembled the familiar places she hiked with her father. Once again, she could be the hunter not

157

the hunted. She thought about all the rabbit traps her father had constructed and wondered if she could make a skilled box herself.

After scrambling back to the top of the embankment, Nhaya found a suitable spot on a log, flipped off her shoes, and began removing the dirt and pebbles that had collected in them from the climb. Then with great care, she took out the leather pouch and pulled open its strings. It was the first time she had seen its contents.

"Looks like you found yer' Indian friends."

Startled, Nhaya looked up to see Ned, the man from the lodge standing a few yards away.

"W-what are you doing here?" She barely got the words passed stammering lips.

"It's a free world." Ned leaned against a tree, tipping the half empty whiskey bottle to his mouth.

Nhaya quickly laced up her shoes and tied the thin strings on the pouch.

"What's in the bag?" Ned wiped his mouth. Carrying his smelly fishing vest with him, he sauntered toward her, the stench of tobacco and liquor reaching her well before he did. She tried to hide the sack behind her, but Ned was quicker than he looked. He reached around and snatched it from her hand.

"Please be careful with that," Nhaya pleaded. "It's nothing you would want. It's just some herbs."

"Don't be in such a rush, Missy. Let's see what you got." Nhaya held her breath.

Ned pulled out a small amount of what resembled dried leaves. He dropped a finger full to the ground. "It's just a bunch of tea." He tipped the bag, spilling more of its contents on the ground.

Enraged, Nhaya landed a hard kick on his shinbone, causing Ned to hop around on his good leg but not hard enough to let go of the bag.

He let out a yelp. "You stupid squaw," he grunted as he bent down to tend his bruised leg.

Nhaya snatched at the pouch from his loosened grip, but still wasn't quick enough to reclaim it. Ned grabbed her jacket and jerked her to the ground.

Nhaya cried out as her shoulder impacted the hard ground. she began to edge away from Ned, scooting backwards on her elbows. She was desperate to put distance between herself and the obviously drunken man.

Ned eyed her He pinned her to the ground rendering her helpless. Ned lowered his face just above hers, "Is this what you want?" He dangled the pouch over her.

"What do you want from me? That is medicine for my sister. It isn't anything to you."

"Well, for starters, how about you show me a little respect?" Suddenly, Ned screamed out in pain. He loosened his grip and rolled over sideways. A long shaft from an arrow protruded from his shoulder. Crying out he and tried to remove it.

Nhaya tried to pull herself up. A hand reached out to help her. "Damien?! Am I glad to see you!"

Ned lay curled up on the ground, holding his arm and whimpering. He looked at Damien and swore. "Hey man, why did you shoot me?"

"Don't take it personal, just evening up the score—an eye for an eye, or in this case, a shoulder for a shoulder, my friend." Damien's eyes held a mischievous glint.

The wounded man breathed out a torrent of cursing and oaths. "I'm not your friend. Who are you anyway?"

Damien strolled over to Ned and inspected his shot. "You shouldn't swear around a lady." He slapped him.

"His name is Ned," Nhaya said, cradling her own arm.

Ned continued to moan as warm liquid ran through his fingers. "I'm gonna bleed to death out here!"

"Ned, my man, looks like you have something that isn't yours." Damien bent over Ned and retrieved Nhaya's bag. He stepped on Ned's wounded arm, ignoring the man's cries of protest. Grabbing the shaft of the arrow, Damien broke off the arrowhead and pulled the shaft through.

Nhaya winced as Ned cried out in renewed pain.

"Get up!" Damien said as he snatched the slivered shaft from Ned's shoulder. "Now, get out of here before you can't."

Ned dragged himself over to a tree and pushed himself up until he could stand. Damien walked over to Ned and lunged at him as if he was going to hit him. Ned cowered, a mere shadow of the threat he posed earlier.

Nhaya bit at her lip, feeling pity for Ned despite herself. "I think he's done, Damien."

Ned limped his way into the covering of the woods. "How do you know him?" Damien asked.

Nhaya brushed herself off and picked up Adam's pack. "I don't. He was at the lodge last night when I got there. He was a bit overly friendly. I guess I didn't do a good enough job of getting away from him."

Damien looked at her, a puzzled look on his face. "So, you didn't know him, but you talked to him?"

"Yes, that's how I knew his name. What's your point?"

"You talk too much. That's the point. And that's why you're in this spot."

"In this spot? You think this is my fault? I don't get you, Damien. One minute you're a hero and the next, you're a real jerk."

Damien laughed at her assumption. "Now you think you know me?"

"No, you're right. I don't," she said disgusted with him.

Damien studied the bag he still held in his hand. "So, she really is still alive, huh?" He held the pouch up and became quiet, retreating into his thoughts.

Nhaya looked up, forgetting her irritation. "Yes, I met her—was with her. Oh, I wished you could have met her. She is everything I imagined."

Damien held the pouch of herbs in his hand as if weighing it. "And you got this from her?"

"You know I did." Nhaya crossed her arms. "She knew what I needed before I told her anything." Nhaya said it with a smug and matter-of-fact tone.

"Of course she did." Damien smiled. "And now your sister—Megan, right? can be saved. That is if it's not too late."

"Why would you say that, Damien? My sister is all I have left."

"You are right I guess I'm not that nice after all. You really need to pay more attention to who talk to."

"Well, there's some valuable advice," Nhaya said with sarcasm. "I'll remember that next time." She held out her hand.

When Damien untied the strings and began poking his finger around in the bag, Nhaya became nervous.

"What else did you and the old lady talk about?"

"All kinds of stuff. Why?" Nhaya kept her eye on the bag. "Did you tell her about me?"

"About you? Why would I do that? Look, this conversation is stupid. I think we should just part ways."

Damien dangled the bag in front of her. "I'll exchange this for the charm."

"What are you talking about, Damien? Just give me the medicine."

Damien pointed to the necklace. "You have no need of it." "This?" She held it up. "Is it why you have been following me?

You know it was my father's. It's the only thing I have left from him. It's not for sale or bargaining. What could it possibly mean to you?"

"It has the power, Nhaya. I saw it with my own eyes! You demonstrated that power on the cliff."

"What are you talking about?" Nhaya cried out, still not believing what he was saying, her fear rising.

"Don't act so naïve. It doesn't become you. You know exactly what I'm talking about. That necklace holds all the power of the last Nez Perce shaman, and her power will be passed on to whoever holds it when she dies."

"But she is still alive. If you think this necklace has some sort of power, you're wrong. It is only a legend."

"So is the old woman…a legend, and yet here she is, in the flesh, alive. Explain to me how you managed to get across that ridge." Damien tossed his quiver's leather strap over his shoulder and prepared to leave.

"I can't."

"And now, I have a job to do." Damien wiped the blood off his arrow tip and slipped it back into his quiver.

"What are you planning, Damien?" She didn't understand until his carefree smile disappeared. When she looked into his eyes, she saw the evil. Her confusion disappeared.

"You're the dark soul. You are the Heyoka."

"She did talk to you."

Nhaya was beginning to understand Damien. He was a loner, with no family and nowhere to go.

"Is that what you are—why you were banned from your tribe?"

Damien drew back his arm but stopped short of striking her. Nhaya flinched.

Damien's voice was bitter. "You don't know anything about me," he hissed. I am a Heyoka and healer. My medicine is strong. Do you know what it is like to hide your face behind the mask and play the fool—making stupid jokes at ceremonies? My powers are just as great as the medicine man's." Damien held his hand against his chest, his face held his pride. "I am proud of what I am. I can heal as well; and I can take away the healing.

They have become afraid of us because they cannot control us. No one controls me."

"What good will taking my necklace do? It's not even from your tribe."

"When I return to my tribe, I will show them I am worthy to be the healer and the leader. I will repay those who opposed me."

"You're crazy, Damien. The necklace has no power."

"Just give it to me and I'll be on my way. Or I will take it from you."

"No, Damien, you will not!"

"Give it to me, now!" Damien yanked open the strings on the pouch.

"Even as bad as you act, I cannot believe you would take the only hope I have of saving my sister's life."

You're the one who put her in danger in the first place, Nhaya. Why didn't you just leave them in the garbage can?"

It took a minute for that to register. . "It was you? You took the mushrooms...not Renée? But how did you—why did you...?" Nhaya couldn't believe her own ears. "You were the one standing in the dark watching me that night when I found them again. I felt a presence."

"I tried to save you some grief, but you didn't get it. Somehow, I hoped we were the same, you and I"

"I'm nothing like you." Nhaya spat out.

Damien sighed. "I know." He began to slowly let the herbs fall silently to the ground.

Nhaya watched in horror as her sister's life slipped away. "Wait! Stop, stop. Here, take it." She quickly pulled the necklace over her head and held it out. "You won't get away with this."

"You get that dialog from a movie?" Damien pulled the prized possession over his neck. He tossed Nhaya the remaining herbs in the sack. "Give my regards to Megan."

CHAPTER TWENTY-TWO

*N*haya choked back angry tears. She refused to believe she could ever be like him, but even now, a part of her had begun to hate. Resisting Damien's evil nature became her driving force, the fuel she needed.

She looked toward the direction of the sun. It was high noon. If she didn't take the path and cut through the woods instead, she could save time. WindWalker had given her the medicine roots, and that meant Megan could still be helped.

She bolted across the trail into the denseness of the forest, running over the uneven ground. She zigzagged through the trees like a deer escaping its attacker; her shoes crushing down choke cherry and buck brush, the thistles tearing into her jeans and flesh.

Each minute seemed an eternity now, every step more difficult than the last. All she could see in her mind was Megan's face and Damien's voice pounding in her head: "You are too late."

No, you are wrong; that is not how it's going to end, Damien. Megan is innocent; she will live.

Nhaya ran like the wind. There wasn't a place on her body that didn't hurt. Staggering in and out of the never-ending uneven terrain of the forest, Nhaya's strength began to wane. How much longer could she continue at this pace? When Adam didn't find her at the lodge, he would start looking for her on the trails. Wouldn't he?

Whether she thought it consciously, it was in the back of her mind. She hoped that Adam would find her.

She had to stop and catch her breath. She looked at her father's watch, shattered and broken. It must have happened when Ned knocked her to the ground. Losing her father's watch along with everything else that had happened, it was just too much. Nhaya wanted to scream and cry, but instead, she gave into the anger and let it drive her forward.

The sun's position appeared to be in the same spot it had been the last time she looked. Now looking around, she had no idea which direction she had come from.

She licked at her chapped lips, but her mouth was too dry to moisten them. Nhaya finally relented and sat down, too tired to argue with herself. Her mind closed to the world around her. *Let's face it Nhaya, you're lost!*

Nhaya picked up a smooth pebble and began rolling it between her fingers again. She never understood why her father did that until he told her. *It helps me keep my mind on task; finding the answer that is already there.* "Okay Nhaya, use your head."

She reached down and felt the softness of the prairie grass she found herself sitting in. The ground was flatter. Her different path had got her to a meadow that she was not familiar with. In her mad dash, she had made it down the mountain! She listened. Somewhere in the distance, she heard what sounded like water. The only fast-moving stream would have been miles away.

She was close to the highway. Nhaya forced herself to get up and moved on trembling legs through the grassland. She had finally cleared the denseness of the forest. A few Douglas-fir trees, mixed with white pines, were all that were left between her and the floor of the valley.

The sound of water continued to grow. But something was wrong. In her mind she drew on images, trying to describe what she heard. The sound was familiar, but out of place; it wasn't a waterfall or a rapid rushing stream. The sound brought to her mind the roaring of an ocean wave breaking on the shore. Then she recognized it. It was the sound of traffic moving back and forth in the distance.

Nhaya raised her head and her hands and cried out, "Thank you Dad. You are with me!"

"I can do this." Nhaya willed her legs to move faster. She recognized the back of Cougar Mountain Lodge and beyond that, the highway. Never had a road looked so beautiful.

Adam could be at the lodge right now. New hope soared as Nhaya began to run. Adam's car was fast, and the way he drove, they could still get back in time.

Nhaya sprinted toward the parking lot and then stopped short in horror. An old grey pickup rolled over the hill a quarter of a mile ahead. As the beat-up truck drew closer, Nhaya could make out a dent on the front fender. That same truck had been parked at the lodge the night before. *It's Ned's*!

The truck slowed and rolled into the lodge parking lot. Sure enough, it was Ned. There was no mistaking him with his bandaged shoulder. He climbed out and staggered into the lodge. Nhaya quickly viewed the parking lot and her heart sank. There was no sign of Adam's car in front. Had he already left?

Not thinking clearly, again, Nhaya stared at Ned's truck sitting there un-attended. To her surprise, the keys were in the ignition, which was the open invitation. She figured he owed her.

The door groaned as she shut it. Peeking over the edge of the rusted hood, Nhaya eyed the door of the lodge. She turned the key The old truck sputtered then started.

"Hey!" Nhaya heard Ned's familiar voice. "That's not yers."

Ned stood on the porch holding a beer in one hand, his mouth gaping.

Panicked, she gunned the engine, both hands gripping the wheel. The pickup lurched and leapt forward, kicking up a rooster tail of smoke and gravel.

Adam had heard the ruckus outside and was not far behind Ned, who was still watching his pickup drive down the road, his mouth spewing all kinds of foul language. "I can't believe it; that stupid girl stole my pickup!" Ned began to cuss again.

"What girl?" Adam's voice commanded.

"That girl! Ned pointed as the truck disappeared. Was it Nhaya?"

"I didn't get 'er name." Ned winced at Adam's grasp. "She was in here last night. Her boyfriend is the one who shot me with his arrow." Ned tried to rub away the resurging pain caused by Adam grabbing it.

"Boyfriend, what boyfriend?" He reached for Ned again. "Whoa with the grabbing," Ned said and stepped away from Adam's outstretched hand. "I don't know. Some Indian who was with her in the woods."

Adam's jaw dropped. "Let me get this straight; you were all together?"

Hearing the conversation, Otis let his apron fall to the floor, heading down the lodge steps. Passing by both Adam and Ned, he headed toward his truck. "Hey," he called out to Adam. "My vehicle's over here, let's go!"

Adam shoved Ned aside. "I'll be back. Don't you move from this spot!" Adam's eyes were ablaze. For a moment and stared at Ned, then headed toward Otis's open side door ignoring Ned's wining.

"Wait, com'on, I wanna come, too. That's my pickup!"

"Maybe we can catch her," Otis said, scrambling in behind the wheel. Both doors slammed shut as the truck took off. Adam shook his head in stunned amazement, watching Ned run along beside the truck holding his injured arm.

Otis braked hard, sliding to a stop, letting three cars pass before heading south on the highway. He and Adam exchanged glances. Adam swore under his breath. If he had been in his car, they would have already caught up.

"Since you got here this morning," Otis commented, "the forest rangers have been searching for her every inch of the forest from here to most of the way up Pine Ridge. I figured that was the way Nhaya would go. I'm sorry, Adam; I had no idea what she was really up to."

Adam's impatience grew by the minute, his voice somber. "I'm sorry, I wish I could give you more information. She didn't leave me with much. Can't this truck go any faster?" Adam could see the truck. He began waving his hands wildly out the pickup window, hoping Nhaya would notice.

Otis chanced a look at the younger man. "I'm the county coroner in these parts, too." He let it sink in. "I've seen a lot of terrible accidents on these roads; people getting in too big a hurry to get on with their vacations.

"Coroner and bartender," Adam said, still keeping his eye on Ned's truck several cars ahead of them. "You get to use your talents often?"

"Well, I seem to always be in demand one way or the other." Otis paused. "People around here have a lot of crazy accidents. Take Ned, for instance. Most folks don't come in shot with an arrow—a gun maybe. As a coroner, I see some pretty bad stuff. Death claims everyone sooner or later, but it's the kids that sadden me most.

"Every once in a while, I get a case that's a real mystery. I was called down to the morgue earlier to take a look at this guy. Rangers found his body at the bottom of High Point Gulley while they were searching for your Nhaya. He had a mark seared deep into the center of his palm like a brand or something. I recognized the markings immediately." Otis pulled out something from his front shirt pocket. "Recognize this?"

"That's Nhaya's necklace! How did you get that?"

"The real question you might want to ask yourself is, from whom?"

Nhaya pressed the pedal to the floor and watched as the speedometer rose, climbing toward 50 miles per hour. Her adrenalin rose to match the speed of the truck. She kept her eyes glued to the black ribbon of highway that stretched out in front of her, the road rising and falling, then curving out of view.

Straining, she managed to stay in the center of the road. Ahead, traffic seemed to be slowing. Nhaya moved over the line to see the problem. It was a logging truck slowing to make a right-hand turn.

It seemed only logical to speed up and pass the few cars that were behind the truck.

Without slowing, Nhaya moved out into the open lane and pressed down on the accelerator. The old truck groaned but responded and increased its speed as she sped past the first two cars. Coming around the bend toward her an oncoming car was directly in her path. Looking up, she stared into the terrified eyes of the approaching driver.

CHAPTER TWENTY-THREE

Several travelers had pulled over to the side of the road to observe the aftermath of the accident, causing traffic to back up for a mile on the narrow winding two-lane highway. The entire area sunk into chaos. Adam and Otis weren't far behind the line of cars. Otis pulled over along with the rest of the on-lookers. They both looked for the truck Nhaya was in. Adam jumped out, his heart racing.

"I'll find a place to park this off the road," Otis called out. He used his two-way radio. "Jim, tell the crew to call off the search for Nhaya. Uh…we might need Life Flight there at the lodge and send an ambulance about twenty miles south on highway 95. There's been a nasty accident. Looks like a head on. Call for traffic control—over." Otis ran as fast as his old legs would carry him to where the crowd was gathering. Adam was nowhere in sight. He could hear people asking all kinds of questions about the nature of the accident.

Otis stopped for a moment to listen to a man repeating how he had miraculously been spared.

"That's right," the owner of the car was saying. "She must have jerked the wheel to miss me because the truck just dodged out of the way right as we were about to collide. I pulled over. There was nowhere else to go but into the woods." The man dabbed at his face with his handkerchief, his voice still shaky.

"I was behind her when that old pickup hit the ditch." Another bystander let out a low whistle. "It went up like a rocket into the air."

"Please sit down, sir." Otis encouraged the man who was the involved driver. "You are in shock, sir. An ambulance will be here shortly. Just sit tight." Otis bent his head and said a short prayer.

"I pulled over immediately," the man kept blabbering, "and came over as fast as I could. The truck grazed that tree"—he pointed to where a pine stood scraped and gouged—"and set down on its wheels. The doors must have flown open upon impact. She was just a girl driving, a teenager, not older than my own niece." The man held his hands to his face and began to sob.

Otis put his arm on his shoulder. "Everything will be okay." Otis reluctantly approached the site. His stomach lurched from the sight of the mangled vehicle. Nhaya was not in the cab.

"Over here," Adam called out.

Nhaya lifted her hand. Something damp and cold laid over her eyes, blocking her vision. She tried to pull it off. Adam removed the napkin for her. She was leaning against him. With some effort, Nhaya lifted her head.

"No you don't. Just lie still," Adam demanded.

Nhaya squinted and tried to figure out who the man was beside her.

"Welcome to the living." Otis squatted down to her level. "Let me take a look at that leg. I was a medic in the war, and I'm the designated doctor in these parts." Then he looked at Adam and arched a brow. "The traffic's backed up quite a ways," Otis told him. "It will take a few minutes to get an ambulance through."

Nhaya groaned. "Where am I?"

"Looks like our girl's coming around. Keep her still, I'll be right back." After another quick peek, Otis disappeared in the direction of the highway to retrieve his emergency medical kit.

"Where am I?" Nhaya tried to get up. "How did I get here?"

"You just took a plane ride." Adam chuckled softly. "The truck you took went off the highway, hit the embankment over there, and then took flight and crashed into the tree. You got ejected. It's a miracle you are still in one piece."

Nhaya's eyes opened wide. "Adam! I thought I was dreaming. Oh, ouch!" She reached for him. Nhaya suddenly remembered the crash. "The man...in the other car...what happened to him? Is he okay? All I can remember...it felt like someone took the wheel from my hand and turned it."

"You must have done it without thinking. Our mind reacts without us knowing sometimes."

Nhaya's mind raced. She recalled her last minutes before impact. The wheel had been yanked from her hand—that she remembered.

Nhaya glanced around for the bag. "I need to find the bag with the medicine. She tried to pull away from Adam. I have to get back."

"Please, just stay still. You could have complications." Adam sat down close beside her and cradled her as best as he could in his arms. He wiped the tears from his eyes.

"I was hoping you would come."

That caused Adam to spring another leak. He wiped his eyes several times before he could talk. "I was in the lodge when you took off in Ned's truck. Otis ran outside to see what Ned was yelling about. We've been following behind you since you left the lodge."

Nhaya flinched from the pain in her shoulder and remembered Ned. "I have to get home."

Otis returned with medical supplies he kept in his truck. He smiled down at Nhaya. "I had the pleasure of meeting Adam last night," he said to Nhaya, making conversation as he began to examine her shoulder.

"Can I have some water?" Nhaya's voice sounded raspy and dry.

Unscrewing the cap from his water bottle, Adam lifted it to her lips. "Drink slowly."

Nhaya choked. "Look, I've just got a bunch of scratches and bruises from my hike over the mountain. I need to get to the hospital." Nhaya lifted her hand and realized she had been clutching the leather pouch.

"I think she is still delirious," Adam commented.

"We will, Nhaya, but first things first." Otis reassured Adam. He placed his hand on her shoulder and took Nhaya's hand. "Your shoulder is dislocated. This is going to smart."

"Look away, Nhaya." Adam held her tight.

She cried out as the bones shifted and slid back into place. Her eyes watered and she remembered Ned's shoulder pain which must have been unbearable when Damien stepped on the arrow to break it and then yanked it out.

Otis pulled a cravat sling from his med kit and secured Nhaya's arm against her chest. He pulled out a preloaded syringe from his bag and gave Nhaya a shot. "This will help with the pain."

"Why didn't you give me that first before you pulled my arm off?"

"She hasn't lost her sense of humor," Adam noted.

"While you were napping," Otis jested back, "I taped up the gash in your leg, but you still need stitches. You must have gotten the cut when you were thrown."

"Adam, I need to get to the hospital…now," Nhaya kept insisting.

Adam brushed loose hair back from her face. "The ambulance will be here soon." Adam was becoming ill at ease.

"No. Not for me. For Megan! She needs this." Nhaya held up the dirty bag wining.

"Megan's okay, Nhaya. I just talked to your mother. I had someone call Monica, too. You're the one who needs the attention now."

"Wha.. what?

"All I know is what your mother told me. Megan got better around five o'clock this morning. Now, please lay back. Everything's good."

"Okay?" *How can that be? Five o'clock*, She repeated the time again.

Nhaya released her death grip... Her head swimming. Megan was okay? She tried to arrange the pieces of her puzzle. She had been in the with WindWalker at that same time.

WindWalker knew she would never get back in time. The herbs, then what were they for?

It was their prayers! Of course. their prayers together. She remembered patches of her father's words: "When people pray together, their prayers become powerful…strong like strings wound together making a rope."

WindWalker knew Megan was already healed before she headed down the mountain. WindWalker believed their prayers would be heard.

Slipping in and out of consciousness, Nhaya tried to pay attention to Adam and Otis.

"Just before you got here, Adam, Ned came into the lodge whining about some crazy fool in the woods he says shot him with an arrow. I gave him something for the pain, patched him up the best I could, and sent him to the small infirmary down the road." Otis shook his head in disgust. "The only thing people used to be concerned about in the forests were the animals. Hunters were smart enough to tell the animals from humans. I should have known Ned was up to something when he followed Nhaya outside last night." Otis shook his head in regret. "I should have offered to drive her back to camp and see to it she got back safe."

"Don't blame yourself," Adam said. "Nhaya wasn't really staying at the campground."

Otis looked at Adam. "I figured that. I also wonder how Ned is connected to the guy found dead in the ravine. Ned has some talking to do."

"Well, you better find him before I do Otis, because he won't be talking much."

"The guy in the morgue was carrying a bow and Nhaya's necklace."

Otis lifted Nhaya's eyelids and checked her pupils. "She has a minor concussion." He finished wrapping her leg in the ace bandage. "Guess that'll have to do. Keep her awake. I'll go direct traffic until help arrives."

Adam gave Otis a firm handshake. "Thank you...for everything." "Oh, by the way"—Otis turned—"if I don't see Nhaya till next year, tell her I did some research last night on the markings scratched on that peace of bone tied to the rawhide string she was wearing. They are Jewish symbols, all right." Otis shook his head. "I can't believe this myself. The mysterious symbols are Jewish for the name God gave himself to his people. When Moses asked him who shall I say sent me. He called himself, 'I Am.' That piece of petrified bone is very old. It has been handed down for many years. It should be in a museum. Relics like that stone offer clues and insight into lost cultures. The writings on that necklace lead me to believe that at least some of the American Indians had a pretty good grasp of the Eternal God."

"You know, Nhaya was out here with some notion that one of her ancestors had a cure to save her sister," Adam told Otis.

"Some things are a mystery, Adam. God works in many ways. Doctors aren't the only ones who corner the market on healing. Ask Nhaya later what happened on the mountain. I'll bet she knows."

Several green and tan ranger trucks were arriving in the parking lot at the lodge. The news went out quickly: "Girl found by rangers." The TV stations set up their cameras in front of the lodge, waiting for any recent news about the accident. Life Flight had arrived and was staged in the parking lot when the ambulance pulled in with Nhaya.

Adam rubbed Nhaya's arm as the ambulance pulled up next to the helicopter. "Ready for another flight? Promise this one will be better." Adam followed beside the stretcher and climbed in with her. "Some of the Kanitsu Park rangers are still out looking for you." Adam said, holding Nhaya's hand. "They have been searching for over six hours."

The helicopter's rotors started.

Nhaya smiled up at him. It didn't matter that she hadn't heard a word he had said, it was enough for her that she had prevailed.

CHAPTER TWENTY-FOUR

*N*haya and Monica sat together in the backseat of the DeSoto. Monica slipped her hand into Nhaya's.

"I'm okay." Nhaya gave Monica a warm smile. "Just a little nervous."

Megan was coming home. Everyone in the car could sense the anticipation.

Miriam and Adam sat in the front seat. "It's hard to believe Megan's coming home today," Miriam said. She pulled up in front of Lake View Hospital. "I've walked these halls here many times." Miriam swept the few straying hairs away from her face along with her happy tears.

Everyone seemed to feel intense at the moment. Nhaya leaned forward and laid her hand on her mother's shoulder. Miriam grasped her fingers, grateful Nhaya was with her.

"I can't believe it's been a whole week…again," Monica commented. "We should still celebrate your homecoming, too, Adam."

Nhaya's hand was at the door handle before Miriam had turned off the key.

"Hold on for a second, Nhaya," Monica said. "Let Adam get your crutches."

"I'm fine now, Monica. I really don't need them. Besides, they kill my shoulder." Nhaya swung her good leg outside and pulled herself up by the open door before Adam could object.

"Jumping out of the car with a bum leg without looking for traffic should earn her a straitjacket, not a driver's permit," Adam mumbled to Miriam.

Monica grabbed her purse. "I'll second that," she chimed in.

Nhaya headed straight for the elevator. It seemed like a year ago that she had pushed that same button bringing her mother the bad news.

"I hope everything is in order," Miriam said, her voice sounding worried. "Sometimes you wait forever to get someone released. I've signed all the papers. The cost to stay in this hospital one day is more than I make in a month." Miriam's words fell silent as the elevator door closed.

Nhaya was the first through its opening doors. The nurses had already packed up Megan's things, and an orderly was there ready to take the rolling table full of flowers, balloons, stuffed animals, and a variety of hospital amenities to their car.

Megan's skin was colorless, but her blue eyes seemed to sparkle when Nhaya bent over and hugged her gently, tears threatening to fall.

"Don't cry again, Ny," Megan begged, tugging at Nhaya's shirt. Nhaya turned around to hide her feelings, again. Luckily, Doctor Telford appeared at the door with Megan's wheelchair ride to the car. "You two are a couple of sorry-looking sights," Doctor Telford Teased Nhaya, "But good sights, nonetheless."

Nhaya excused herself. "I need to use the restroom." She grabbed a Kleenex and dabbed her eyes.

Nhaya stared at herself in the medicine cabinet mirror. With a few exceptions, the person staring back at her looked the same. No one would suspect the change in her. But she was different inside.

In twenty-four hours so much had happened to her on the mountain, good and bad.

When she finally hobbled out of the bathroom, she found Adam and Monica waiting in the corridor for her. Adam touched the side of Nhaya's face.

"It's not as bad as it looks guys," she said and smiled.

"Still looks awful sore to me." Monica added.

"Thanks, Monica. You always know how to make a girl feel pretty." Nhaya covered her bruised and still-swollen eye with her hair. "Let's just get out of here."

Moving outside, Nhaya stood on the hospital's front steps. Below her, the gutters that lined the streets were still clogged with debris from last week's storm. She looked toward the east and thought of WindWalker.

Adam stood behind her and wrapped his arms around her waist. It felt good. She rested her hands on his hands and leaned into his embrace.

A nurse wheeled Megan down the ramp and out to their waiting car. Miriam handed Nhaya the car keys and sat in the passenger's seat.

"Really, Mom?"

"You're gonna drive?" Megan asked Nhaya.

"Do you think it's a good idea—I mean, so soon, Mrs. Winters?" Adam said.

"She is going to have to learn to drive right sometime," Miriam explained. "It's a ten-minute drive. Besides, I will be right here if she even thinks about passing anyone."

"Just take it slow, Nhaya," Adam put his two cents worth in.

"Are you sure, Mom?" Nhaya asked again.

"You tell me, Honey. You maneuver our stairs pretty well, and the doctor gave his okay to release you. You think you're ready?"

Nhaya slid into the driver's seat, adjusted the rearview mirror, and pulled the seatbelt tight. "This is just too much!" Nhaya glanced in the rearview mirror.

"Besides your mother, you have three backseat drivers, Nhaya," Monica told her.

"Funny, guys." Her heartbeat quickened as she shifted into first gear. "Things have changed since you've been away, Megan."

The traffic moved faster at six o'clock, but Nhaya didn't think twice or worry. Her confidence soared. She knew a car was in her future. After all, her mother couldn't continue to drive her everywhere.

"Use your blinker before you turn," Adam directed Nhaya from the back seat.

"Even turning on to our deserted street?" Nhaya asked.

The DeSoto pulled up to the front of their house. Home never looked better. Adam got out and opened Miriam's door first.

"You looked a little nervous there in the backseat." Miriam laughed.

Adam couldn't deny it. Then he spoke to Megan. "Come here." Adam scooped Megan up and carried her across the lawn. "You are getting too heavy for me." Adam laughed. He faked a loud groan and staggered up the front steps.

Megan giggled with delight.

"Be careful, Adam," Miriam called after him. "She's still sick."

"No, I'm not." Megan giggled. She hugged his neck harder.

Nhaya drove up the long driveway and parked the DeSoto in the garage with no trouble. After turning off the key, she stayed in the car. She ran her hands around the steering wheel, still filtering things through her mind.

Monica moved into the front seat with her.

"Thank you for everything you did, Monica," Nhaya said. "I can't believe it's over. I just wanted to say I am sorry you had to go to my house and take care of something I should have done. If I had everything to do all over again, It would change a lot."

"Hey, you were a little busy." Monica rubbed Nhaya's arm. "From my perspective, you did everything you could have done."

"I put you in danger. You didn't know how dangerous Damien was."

"Damien? Nhaya, who's Damien?"

"You know, Damien—the guy you talked to who came to my house. You told him about Meg and where I was going."

"Nhaya, no one came to your house when I was there."

"You never met him?"

"No, who is he?"

Nhaya was dumbfounded. "Then how did he know where I was? I never told him anything."

"Told him what? You're losing me again, Nhaya."

"This guy I met at camp. I thought he was with the rest of the Nez Perce group who were at camp this year. He must have followed me home and somehow found out where I lived. I saw him on the mountain. He followed me up there, too. But I have no idea how he knew about Megan or why I was there. He told me you told him."

"Boy, Nhaya, that is scary. He was a stalker?"

"He was a lot more than that, Monica. He suddenly showed up on the road I was walking on after I ran out of gas."

"And you actually got into the car with him?"

"I did." Nhaya looked at her.

They both sat in silence.

Nhaya and Monica left the garage and entered through the back door and continued through the kitchen. Miriam busied herself with a pan on the stove. They found Adam upstairs with Megan.

"Will you take Monica home, Adam? That is, when you are through teasing Megan?"

"Sure, I'll run her home."

"Don't go, Adam," Megan begged.

Nhaya sensed a new intimacy when she looked around the room. "I see you have your friend again, Adam. It didn't take long for her to warm up to you."

"She's a heartbreaker," Miriam warned Adam coming into the room. She set the warm glass of milk down on the lamp stand next of us," Miriam's fingers rubbed at her forehead. "You need to sleep in your own bed tonight. Maybe you can sleep in the spare bedroom downstairs tomorrow when you take your nap."

"Can you stay with me till I fall asleep, Nhaya?"

Nhaya smiled, handed Megan her doll, and sat next to her on the bed.

"Be back in a few." Adam kissed Nhaya's cheek.

Nhaya's face flushed. Megan covered up her mouth to suppress her giggle.

"Welcome back home. Thank you for helping out our family, Adam." Miriam slipped out of the room.

"Goodnight, Megan." Monica slipped out of the room, too.

Nhaya regained her composure from Adam kissing her in front of everyone. "See you in a few minutes."

Megan lifted her rag doll's red checkered skirt. "What happened to Gretchen?"

"Well, I washed her this morning."

"She does look better." Megan gave her doll a big kiss. "And she smells better, too. Did you like camp?"

Nhaya thought for a moment. "I learned something about the moon. Do you know what a crescent moon looks like?"

"Sure, it's the one the little boy sits on when he's fishing in the sky."

"Yes, that's right. Well, the moon is almost full tonight. If the little boy tried fishing tonight, he would fall off."

Megan giggled.

Nhaya walked over and opened her window. "When the moon is becoming full like it is now, it is called a waxing gibbous. When a full moon goes to a half moon, it's called a waning gibbous."

"Wayne who?" Megan asked.

Nhaya laughed. "I guess you aren't ready for scientific names quite yet."

"I'm glad I didn't go to camp; it's way too hard," Megan said.

Nhaya pulled the rocking chair over next to the open window. She picked up Megan with her blanket and they cuddled together.

Nhaya rocked her back and forth, quietly humming the tune her father had taught her.

"I see the moon; the moon sees me." Megan began to sing the words with Nhaya.

"How do you know that song, Meg?"

"Daddy sometimes sang it to me at night."

Nhaya chose her words carefully. "Megan, Mom told me you saw an Indian woman at the hospital."

"I saw her in my dreams. Mom said she must have been an angel." Megan yawned.

Nhaya waited for her to say more. She carried Megan across the room and lay down beside her.

"What did she look like, sweetie?" "Who?"

"The angel."

"She had a long white braid and a big black bird was sitting on her shoulder." Megan rolled over and looked at her.

Nhaya was at a loss for words. "Do you ever miss Daddy, Meg?"

"Sometimes when I'm sad or afraid, I feel like he's near me. Maybe she knows Daddy."

"You mean the angel?" Megan didn't answer her.

"Maybe she does, honey. Maybe she does."

Nhaya slipped outside Megan's bedroom door and went downstairs. Her eyes were wet with tears. She couldn't recall ever crying so much.

Now it seemed Megan remembered her father, too.

Nhaya's heart was light as her feet hobbled down the stairs. Adam's face lit up as soon as Nhaya's presence entered the kitchen. Nhaya slipped behind her mother, giving her a quick hug as she reached out and opened the refrigerator door.

"That was a fast trip back, Adam." She paused. "Oh, I forgot, that car of yours can sprout wings," she teased him.

Adam looked sheepish when Miriam shot Adam a look.

Opening three bottles of pop from the refrigerator, Nhaya handed them out. "Don't worry, Mom"—Nhaya's devilish eyes were on Adam—"he's a good driver."

The three of them sat down at the kitchen table in a peaceful silence. Adam immediately chugged half of his bottle; Nhaya sipped at hers.

Miriam spoke first. "Thanks for helping us get Megan upstairs," Miriam told Adam again. She set her half-consumed bottle down and walked toward the back porch. "It looks like one of my coworker's was kind enough to leave us a pot of soup. Everyone has been so supportive to us. Will you help me bring this pot into the kitchen? You are going to stay for dinner, right?"

Adam eagerly carried in the heavy black cast iron pot and set it on the stove.

"Yes, please stay, Adam," Nhaya added.

"Sure, I never turn down a good meal. So what's for dinner? I could eat a cow."

Miriam lifted the heavy lid. "Well, it's not a cow." There was a long pause. "Good Lord, I think its mushroom soup!"

Nhaya looked at her mother. "I'll call for pizza."

"And I'll buy," Adam spoke up looking for the phone. "What does everyone want on it?"

"Anything but mushrooms!" both Nhaya and her mother chimed in unison.

Everyone broke into laughter.

CHAPTER TWENTY-FIVE

*O*ver the next few days, life returned almost back to normal. Enjoying the cooler evening breeze, Nhaya sat quietly in the porch swing as Adam gently pushed it with his feet.

She thought about her wanting Damien dead. It troubled her that she herself could be so cold hearted. Over the last few nights, her dreams became nightmares about Damien. Damien would appear before her, wearing the ceremonial mask. One by one, everyone who opposed him fell, touched by death at his hand. She sat a little closer to Adam appreciating the comfort of being beside him.

Adam had remained by her side lately, sometimes too attentive. He was pushing Nhaya for details about things she just didn't want to talk about, things she would rather leave untouched. Although comfortable with him, the silence had grown heavy between them. She knew he was waiting for answers that she was not sure she was ready to give.

He had pointed out several times before that she was keeping things from him, things that were putting distance between them— hurting their relationship. Looking at him again, she sighed softly.

She knew she would eventually have to break open the vault of her heart and let him in, to allow him to at least try and understand.

Adam broke the silence. "I've been patient. It's been a week, Nhaya. Now we need to talk." He looked at her when he spoke, his voice quiet, yet firm. "What happened on the mountain?"

Nhaya didn't know where to start. "I'm sorry I lost your backpack," Nhaya said, her fingers intertwined in her lap.

"My backpack? Is that what you think I care about?"

"No." She shook her head. "I know it isn't. I just don't want to relive everything right now."

"Well, let's start with this." Adam carefully removed her necklace from his pocket. "I forgot to give it to you this with all that was going on."

Nhaya looked at Adam in disbelief. "How did you get this?"

His eyes were both cold and hurt. "You need to be more careful who you give it to."

Adam's words offended her. Nhaya took the necklace from his hand. "It's not what you think."

"Then tell me what it is. I know I've been gone for over a year, and we've only spent a few hours together since I got back." He lowered his gaze, hiding his eyes.

Adam was jealous. She faced him, "I'm sorry. I didn't imagine you would think I was with someone else." She touched his face softly, allowing her hand to trace the curve of his jaw. "I have been such the fool. You have been so good to me. I feel I've taken you for granted, Adam."

Adam let down his guard. He inhaled, and his words exploded from him in a rush. "I had to work that night, Nhaya. I would have lost my job if I'd just taken off. Jobs are hard to come by up here. It was torture for me—just watching you leave, then simply waiting."

Nhaya remembered her feelings again the night she boarded the bus. She had felt betrayed by him, too.

He pulled her close. "So now I'm telling you." He lifted her face with a knuckle, forcing her to look at him. "I was just so afraid you would find someone when I was gone. I thought he was it?" He smiled weakly. "I thought you had a thing going on with him."

"His name is Damien, and no, there was nothing going on between us."

"I should have never allowed you to leave without me. But you just weren't making any sense at the station that night. I should have quit right there on the spot. Next time, I swear, I'll listen better and not judge you."

Adam's words began to melt the coldness in her heart and the protective shield that had wrapped itself around her.

Adam continued with his plight. "So, when I finally made it to the lodge, Otis was patching up some guy who was going on about getting shot with an arrow." He took a breath, then finished. "I guess that turned out to be Ned, the guy's truck you took."

Nhaya remembered and hung her head.

"I asked Otis about you. He was a pretty informative guy." Adam perked up. "We got to talking. That's when the search for you started. I took off looking around the area myself for anyone I could find who might have seen you. When I returned to the lodge, Ned ran outside screaming about someone stealing his truck. That's when we followed you."

Nhaya looked at him, swallowing hard, and held up the necklace. "How did you find this then?"

"I didn't. Otis did at the morgue."

"At the morgue? From Damien? How, uh…how did he die?" Nhaya stammered.

Adam looked up. "I think Otis told me he fell off some cliff, and he had your necklace in his hand."

Nhaya was silent. Overwhelmed by his statement, she bowed her head, hiding her face in her hands. "I didn't give it to him, Adam," she said quietly. "He took it from me. He was interested in this, not me."

"Who was this guy to you?"

She blew loose strands of hair from her face. "I'll give you the short version. Damien saw me at camp. I had the necklace on. He

187

recognized it as being important to him. He decided he wanted it bad enough to take it from me."

Adam bristled with anger. "So where does Ned come into this story?"

"Ned was in the woods, too, but not for me. He was just drinking. I ran into him by accident on my way back. He—Ned, wanted to see what I had in the pouch that I was carrying. I became afraid and tried to run. But he grabbed at me and I fell down. That's how I hurt my shoulder. He took the herbs. Damien must have been watching."

"So Damien took the necklace from—"

"Damien took the herbs from Ned after he shot him with an arrow and used them to force me to give him the necklace."

"Nice guy."

"He knew who I was looking for. He told me the necklace had great power and that I didn't deserve it. He could have taken the necklace from me, but I think he was afraid of something. Maybe because of the stories handed down about its mysterious power."

"You found the woman you were looking for?"

"She gave me this." Nhaya removed the pouch of herbs from her pocket. "Megan didn't need them after all I did. I needed it to believe that Megan would be healed without them. Adam, it was the Great Grandfather Spirit—God—that healed Megan. WindWalker and I prayed together that morning before I left her. She had the faith to believe Megan would be healed. She was once the holy woman in her tribe. There is so much more I want to learn about her and her faith."

"So do you think it is true about the power of the necklace?", Adam asked her.

"Do really want to know what I think." Nhaya looked at him. "When I crossed that ledge on the mountain, I lost my footing. I can't explain it, but a wind just came up out from nowhere and pressed me against that wall. It held me there until I regained my footing. Damien was there, he saw it happen. He was sure it was because of the necklace." Nhaya shook her head just as fascinated by the telling him.

She continued, "I wasn't sure what to think. But I do know this; I didn't have the necklace when I found my way off the mountain, even though I was hopelessly lost.

"Then there was the whole truck thing. It sure wasn't my hand that turned the steering wheel and saved me. I wasn't in possession of the necklace then either. Does that answer your question?"

She asked, allowing Adam to draw his own conclusion.

They both sat in silence for a while, each thinking over what had been said.

Adam stood and tucked his shirt in. He let out a sigh. "That is the craziest story I have ever heard told. If I hadn't seen some of the things with my own eyes, I wouldn't believe any of it. But that being said…" He rested his hands on both of Nhaya's arms. "Listen to me; this is what matters. I'm crazy about you. I have been since we were kids. I just thought you knew."

Adam sucked in a deep breath as if relieved from a burden. "At least I know I am still in the lead for your affections."

Adam looked intently at Nhaya, his eyes bright, full of wonder and love. He captured her face in his hands and waited. "Do I really have to do this alone?"

Nhaya met his lips in a kiss.

CHAPTER TWENTY-SIX

*N*haya watched Adam drive away. She left the door open, still enjoying the feel of his kiss on her lips and the rush of anticipation she got when he lifted her face to his.

She had been nervous as Adam closed the distance between them. She wasn't sure what to expect. When Justin had come that close, she had expected a game of cat and mouse, thinking he would tease her while hoping he would try to kiss her. Adam's kiss was her first real kiss.

Adam's passion scared her. Sure, she wanted him to care for her, but something felt wrong. She wasn't ready for anything more than that, and she wasn't sure if she wanted him to wait until she was ready.

Nhaya closed the door and flopped down on the couch, missing her father more now than ever.

"Are you hurting?" Miriam asked, sitting down next to Nhaya. "It's eight o'clock. You can take more medication."

Nhaya looked up in surprise because her mother hadn't immediately asked about Adam. "No, Mom, I'm okay." Nhaya smiled at her. "Mom, thanks."

"For what?"

"Just being my mother." Nhaya surrendered to the warmth of her mother's arms wrapping around her and enjoyed sitting in comfortable silence.

Nhaya spoke, "I was just thinking about Adam."

"He is a nice young man." Her mother agreed.

"It's just—I'm confused about how I feel."

"That's all right, Nhaya, so are most teens at your age. Is he moving too fast for you?"

Nhaya tossed her head, brushing the hair back from her face. "Mom, what does it actually feel like to be in love?"

"That's a great question. But are you really questioning how you feel about Adam?"

"I guess."

"I think Adam may have the beginnings of love for you." She smiled. "He's had a crush on you since forever, but that doesn't mean you're obligated to return those feelings." Miriam touched her ring finger unconsciously as she spoke. "Don't worry, you will figure things out. Just give yourself time."

Nhaya was asleep when Miriam gently shook her. She stretched. "How long have I been sleeping." She rubbed the sleep from her eyes.

"About two hours. I made some iced tea for us." Miriam handed Nhaya a tall glass.

Nhaya wrapped her hands around the glass.

"Do you want to sit with me on the swing for a while?"

She followed her mother to the porch and watched as Miriam piled Megan's dolls in a corner of the swing and sat down. She patted the space beside her.

Nhaya sat next to her.

"It was nothing but a miracle that Megan recovered." Miriam's bared feet gently moved the swing back and forth.

"I was told that nothing more could be done for her. When the doctor called me at five that morning, I thought the worst. I fell to my knees, Nhaya."

"And gave thanks to God when he gave me the good news instead."

"Megan is awake…and asking for a cookie…a blasted peanut butter cookie.'"

Miriam began to laugh. "I asked him what had changed. He told me that no medicine known to man could have pulled Megan through."

"Mom, I have so much I want to tell you. I was praying for Megan at the same time she got healed."

"Adam told me you had left him alone and took a bus back to the camp. He said you had to find someone to help Megan."

"Mom What does Nimiipuu mean?"

Miriam paused and reflected before answering. "It's from the old language. It means Nez Perce."

"Someone called me by that name." Nhaya said, hoping for an opening to tell her all that had happened.

"Did your father ever tell you about your great, great grandmother, that she was a holy woman?"

Nhaya looked up, surprised. "Mom, I've had this same dream over and over for as long as I can remember about this woman." She eyed her mother and when she saw that she was waiting, she continued.

She's an old Indian Woman dressed in beautiful Indian wear. Her hair is white and in a braid. She carries a long pipe and; Nhaya waited… I saw her at camp this week." She stood in front of me and said something."

"That's impossible, Nhaya. She can't still be alive."

"You know her? I went to the mountains to find her after I left the hospital that night. I knew she could help Megan because she was at the camp.

She said, *"you see me and you will come."*

Miriam sat back with a look of bewilderment "Nhaya, I'm sure you're mistaken. WindWalker would have to be well over 150 years old by now."

"That was her name, mom! I swear—I'm not lying. She was beautiful and she was real. She wore the same clothes on the mountain that she wore at camp, and she was in the picture I saw at the Cougar Mountain Lodge last week. Otis, the barkeeper, told me her name was WindWalker."

Nhaya became more and more animated as she described her time with time with WindWalker. "Mom, she knew why I was coming to see her! We sat and ate at her camp." Nhaya started coughing and her face began to sweat.

Miriam she could see that Nhaya was still in pain. "You need your meds. Doctor Telford said you were not out of the woods yet. Let's get you up to a nice bath. There will be plenty of time to talk about this later."

Nhaya obediently headed toward her room. She was tired and her leg was starting to throb. Miriam helped her up the stairs. Miriam began pulling off her shoes.

Nhaya unbutton her shirt. "Honestly, Mom, I can manage this," Nhaya felt embarrassed.

"Okay. Then I'll draw you a nice hot bath."

"You were right about my leg. Can you get my medicine, too, please?"

After checking on Megan, Miriam returned with a glass of water and Nhaya's pills. She picked up her daughter's jeans with two fingers with disgust. "You girls will wear the same clothes until they fall off your body. I'll take these to the trash. They are filthy and have holes in them."

As Miriam shook out the jeans something fell on the carpet. She picked it up. "What's this? Oh- it must be Adam's ring," she teased Nhaya through the open bathroom door.

Nhaya looked out to see her mother holding the gold ring between her thumb and index finger. "Um, no, actually I found it at camp."

Miriam used her apron to clean off more of the dirt. When she examined the markings on the inside, her breath caught, the color draining from her face. "Where exactly did you get this, Nhaya?" Miriam entered he bathroom. A strange look on her face. Miriam slipped it on her thumb.

"It was weird, Mom. A hawk had it in his beak. He dropped it in front of me, then just flew away."

Miriam sank down onto the bed, speechless.

"Do you know what the markings mean?" Nhaya called out from the bathroom unaware of her mother's reaction to the ring. After a long silence, Nhaya stepped out of the tub.

"Mom?" Nhaya grabbed her robe from the hook on the door and put it on.

"As a matter of fact, I do." Then she laughed. "I do. That's what I said to your father when I put this ring on his finger. I tried to draw a pair of wings. Your dad's given Indian name is Winter Hawk—'*to protect*.' Miriam read the words. Tears made silent treks down her face. "Your father etched that inscription inside it. His vow to me was to always protect me and our family."

"Nhaya"—Miriam laughed through her tears—"this is your father's ring. He lost it years ago when we were camping." Miriam hugged the ring to her bosom and closed her eyes reliving the memory.

"What? Dad's wedding ring?" Nhaya walked over and stood near her mother.

"Sit.," her mother patted the bed.

They sat together, their legs crossed, facing each other like little girls on a sleepover. "Tell, me how you found the ring, Nhaya. Tell me everything," Miriam said.

"A hawk flew into a window at camp when I was waiting to see the counselor. It came in for food that was left on the counselor's desk. It dropped the ring from its beak to eat." Nhaya reached out and brushed the ring with her finger. "And you're telling me it's Dad's ring?"

"It's not unusual for birds to gather objects. They love shinny objects and often use them in their nest building."

"Yeah, but mom, Dad's ring? And I found it? Or I should say it was given to me by a bird?"

Miriam sat for a moment, then said, "How strange…there was a red-tailed hawk outside the kitchen window the day of the storm. It was peculiar to see such a hawk this far north. It was just sitting on the clothesline pole and no matter how hard the wind blew; it didn't fly away."

Nhaya smiled. She knew it was the same hawk. Her mother would never believe it this one.

"Mom," she ventured, "how did you know you loved Dad?"

Miriam looked down at the ring again. "I had been so angry with your father the day he lost this. I couldn't believe he would take it off. He told me later he needed to wash the fish smell off his hands and had left it by the stream.

We went back to the place but never found it." She shook her head against the memory. "I was so angry. It was only a ring, Nhaya. I handled it wrong. I was young."

Miriam looked away as if she was embarrassed by the confession. "I wouldn't care if I ever had a ring. If only I could have your father back here with me, even for a day, would mean everything to me." Her eyes brimmed then overflowed with tears.

"I miss him, too, Mom." She was beginning to understand how much her mother's life had been shattered, too. Nhaya hugged her After her mother's confession, Nhaya realized her parents must have had problems of their own.

Nhaya slipped into Megan's room, closing the door behind her. Thankfully, Megan was playing outside with her new doll. Nhaya knew there were more secrets somewhere, and she had questions that still needed to be answered. Perhaps they were inside her mother's cedar chest.

She removed the dolls that covered the top of the trunk and dug through Megan's baby clothes. Her anticipation grew when she saw the black leather photo album near the bottom.

She pulled it out, sat down on the floor, and began searching the pages. There were old black and white photos of her father and his family, neatly pasted on black paper. Nhaya flipped through the newspaper clippings. A few articles were written about her father, taking the championship four years in a row with his bow.

Nhaya laughed at the photo with her Aunt Bessie and her mother together holding hands when they were young. On the back page, she found a picture of her father sitting in the rocking chair on the front porch. She held it close to her heart.

She didn't find what she was looking for. WindWalker was nowhere in any of the albums. Slowly she placed everything neatly back. Then she laid the necklace in a safe place and latched the trunk. Her mother was right. The necklace wasn't to wear.

Nhaya took the picture of her father outside with her. She sat on the edge of the porch as Megan played happily with Gretchen. It was as if Megan had never been sick. Nhaya twisted a strand of her hair.

"Why the long face?" Miriam watched Nhaya from the open door.

"Oh, nothing. I decided to look at some old pictures of Dad." She held a picture of the young man.

"He sure was a handsome guy."

Miriam took Nhaya's hand and led her into the bedroom she'd shared with her husband. From a wooden box on the closet floor, she produced an old worn picture. It was of an old Indian woman.

"Mom, that's her! That's WindWalker! She's the one I met in the meadow!" Nhaya stared at the photo. A row of animal teeth circled the woman's neck, and in her hand was the walking stick.

"She was my great, great grandmother," Miriam explained.

"Yours, not Dad's?" Nhaya looked shocked.

Miriam took the picture and studied it. Nhaya could tell by its worn edges that her mother had held it many times.

"I have Native American blood running through my veins, too, you know." This time her smile was genuine. "I just never talk about it anymore." Miriam put her arm around Nhaya's shoulder. "I had tried to wipe away the past."

"But why, Mom? I don't understand."

"It's complicated," Miriam said, and patted the bed. "Sit down, Nhaya. People can be cruel. We will never be accepted if we continue to follow our old customs. We moved to Dover to get away from all the prejudice and narrow-minded people in Montana. Your Aunt Bessie decided to stay there. She was married to a vary wealth rancher. I think she has lived to regret her choices though...

We can still be ourselves and be proud of our heritage, Mom. You have an education and a good job. No one is looking down on you," Nhaya said.

"I realize that. I've had a lot of things out of perspective, including our relationship."

"Like what?" Nhaya wanted to know.

"Like I think you believe I love Megan more than you."

Nhaya suddenly felt uncomfortable. She wasn't ready for her mother's truth. "It's okay, Mom, I understand. Megan is younger and needs more attention."

"No, that's not it at all. The truth is, you remind me so much of your father and sometimes it just hurts. I loved him so much, and I miss him terribly. And even though it wasn't his fault, I've been angry with him that he left us alone and broke his promise to protect us I had no one to turn to when I needed to vent. I misplaced my anger. It landed on you. You see, he promised to protect me. This ring brought that back to me again. I have cried my eyes out and hating myself for not being able to get past it."

Nhaya thought about her own attitude and grabbed her mother's hands, intertwining their fingers. "Mom, I'm sorry, too.

I haven't been very loving either. I never understood what you were going through. I was too busy feeling sorry for myself. I guess everyone has things they regret, huh?"

"You are pretty smart for a teenager."

Nhaya eyed her mother.

"That was supposed to be funny, Nhaya." Miriam laughed.

"Oh." Nhaya hadn't seen that side of her mother in a long time. She smiled and unlaced her bracelet, tying it around her mother's wrist. "I think you should have this. I made it at camp for you." Nhaya ran her finger across the beads. "The symbols stand for wisdom."

Miriam examined the bracelet. "You know, years ago I made one just like this, only I chose the symbol for bravery. I think it should belong to you. Would you like to see it?"

"You still have it, really?"

"I have a lot of precious things." Miriam bent over the bed and re-opened the box that held WindWalker's picture and brought out the small bracelet. She handed it to Nhaya.

"There's something else I think you deserve." Miriam produced a white tipped eagle feather. It's your father's. I know he would want you to have it."

The golden eagle feather is a symbol of honor, the highest badge of courage for a brave. It was also used in healing ceremonies. No prayer was complete without the presence of the eagle feathers. Nhaya held it up with a sense of wonder and pride. Miriam's reflective smile told Nhaya her mom was proud of it, too.

Miriam studied the photo again. "Our great, great grandmother was a healer, it was a special gift given to her. Many in her lineage were gifted healers as well. WindWalker's gifts were used to help many tribes. She was so well-known that she was turned into legend or what we call today as a Saint. Only most people didn't understand where her real power came from. They called it magic." She sighed.

Miriam looked at Nhaya, assessing her. "I didn't want any part of it. I guess I was afraid of the responsibility. I was wrong to keep it from you. I chose for you, too."

Nhaya remembered what WindWalker had told her. "You must choose for yourself." It all made sense.

"Mom, I know you don't want to believe I saw WindWalker, but how do you explain the picture at the lodge that I recognized from my dream and the woman who came to camp being the same person? I went to Pine Ridge to find her, and I did. She led me to her tent. She used the same ceremonial pipe that was in the picture. We prayed together. It was five in the morning when I left to come back down the mountain.

You said Dr. Telford called right at that time and gave you the news that Megan is alive and well, Mom. Only God can heal something that can't be healed by medicine."

Miriam sat silent, contemplative.

"Look, WindWalker gave me these herbs." Nhaya reached in her pocket and found the pouch. She opened it and showed her.

"WindWalker told me, they were for healing. I thought that she was saying that Megan would be healed after I brought her the herbs, but WindWalker already knew Megan was okay. I crashed the car trying to get home before it was too late to give them to her. By that time Megan was already well... well!"

"Life is full of he unexplainable. And yes, I guess I do believe you." Miriam smiled at her and stroked her cheek. "How could I not."

"She called me Nimiipuu and told me to walk the 'Red Road'. I told her I would. I've guessed by now it's not a real place."

"Yes, The Red Road. All of our ancestors believe it is about our walk in life, the road of balance. Each of us must walk our own path, Nhaya. Walking in humility and loving our fellow man, forgiving them as well as ourselves."

"She told me about my path. She said it was 'North-South'." Nhaya began to understand what WindWalker was saying. "So the north means patience and purity, and the south road is discipline with direction."

"Yes, then that's your Red Road."

"What WindWalker told me protected me and helped me get back home. I want to be faithful to my promise to her and to the Great Spirit. That means God, right?"

Nhaya looked at her mother and smiled. "Can we go back to church again? The best camp I ever went to was that church camp, when we lived in Coeur d'Alene."

"I think that is a very good idea," Miriam said. "We could all benefit from that. Maybe it's time we make some new beginnings… for all of us next Sunday."

"Maybe we could meet up with Monica in Sandpoint."

"Do you want to see Renée?"

"I don't think that is such a good idea about Renée. I have some crow to eat first. I'd rather do that without an audience."

Miriam looked at Nhaya. "Something I should know about?"
"Just camp stuff, Mom. I was a real jerk."

"Oh!" Miriam exclaimed. "Look out the window. I think that's the hawk that's been hanging around here lately." She pointed to the large bird perched on the fence.

Nhaya walked to the window and watched the hawk take flight.

She wondered if she would ever see it again. He was a part of her, now, too.

Megan appeared at the bedroom door. She had been listening to their conversation and suddenly began to cry.

"What's the matter, Megan?" Miriam scooped her up and set her on the bed.

"I don't want Nhaya to eat any crow. They would taste terrible bad."

"Megan." Both Nhaya and her mother began to laugh hysterically. "That is something someone says when they have to give an apology," Nhaya told her. "What's an apology?"

"Girl, did anyone ever tell you, you ask too many questions?

EPILOGUE

*I*t was dawn. The sun's rays came through Nhaya's window, bringing the promise of a new day. Nhaya was already dressed. She had finished packing the night before.

"You must choose." Even her mother had said it.

She was eighteen now. She had chosen her path. The one God had set for her. She had found her real hero, her Constant. She was told He had chosen her before she was even born.

The road hadn't been easy. As promised, she began her walk on her "Red Road" of patience, purity, discipline, and direction. Her patience became her will to wait until she was eighteen to begin her own journey. She had remained pure in spite of Adam's insistence. He wanted to marry her and start a family right away. She loved him dearly, but marriage wasn't for her.

She found it was only by staying true to God's word that she could stay on that right path. She found strength in one of her favorite verses from the Old Testament in the Bible. "Thy word is a lamp unto my feet, and a light unto my path." God had promised to guide her and He had.

Nhaya slipped out the front door. It was too painful to say her goodbyes again.

The Great Spirit now lived in her, leading her to others. Nhaya had learned the secret to WindWalker's greatness. It wasn't magic that drew others to her; it was her faith and love for others.

Nhaya smiled. She still had one stop to make. She had to see Otis, wanting to tell him he had been right. Like the universe, God is constant and the same throughout the ages. His love never fails. She would be a demonstration of that.

Her journey was just beginning.

The End

IN APPRECIATION

With appreciation I want to thank you, Jon, my beloved husband for being my constant through our life together and in my writing.

The journey and completion of this story was greatly enhanced by the encouragement and ideas from my good friends and writers, Bridget, Valerie, and Becky.

The special piece of artwork on the cover (the necklace) was designed by my granddaughter, Mikayla. You are beautiful and loved.